# GHOST STORY

## Peter Nash

For the wonderful Joseph.

Fomite

Burlington VT

ISBN-13: 978-1-959984-62-7
Library of Congress Control Number: 2024938062

Fomite
58 Peru Street
Burlington, VT 05401
www.fomitepress.com

09-16-2024

For Annie, Isaiah, Ezra, and Kyra

For MRN

If it's possible to have a thought without a word or an image, without time and space—complete, created by me, a revelation of what remains hidden in me (and from me) but suddenly appears, if it could be born so clearly for all to see, without origin, without any effort of breath, of tone of voice, of rhythm or hesitation, without vision even, emerging like a normal thought, or more than a thought: a thing—if such a thing could exist, then I'd like to tell a story.

~Beatriz Bracher

Every love story is a ghost story.

~David Foster Wallace

SHE SENT ME THERE TO follow him, to see where he ate and drank—and with whom. She sent me there to prove her right. Of course she knew she was right when she sent me. She knew what I would find.

The night before I left for England I met Mary at their apartment on Morningside Drive. We'd known each other for years, so that there was little pretense between us when she opened the door. She said I looked thinner, pale; she said I looked tired. Her sons, Ivan and Jack, were watching television in the living room, a room I'd occasionally slept in when Richard was away. Taking my umbrella, she poured me a glass of wine from a large green bottle by the sink, then led me down the hallway to the living room, with its books and kilims and darkly-shaded lamps, where we settled ourselves on the couch behind the boys, who lay sprawled on the floor in their pajamas. They were of an age when we could speak freely with one another, say anything we felt without arousing their attention and having to explain.

We'd always spoken freely with one another—at least she'd spoken freely with me, a fact that, until that evening, had seemed much the same thing. For reasons I'd never quite plumbed, I'd rarely felt the need to talk while in the presence of others, to pronounce or profess, to tease or joke, to lay claim (as of some physical territory) to my beliefs and predilections, as most seemed wont, if not eager, often anxious, to do. At gatherings with friends or colleagues, even alone with Mary, when Richard was away, or with Mary and her brother, Ian, when he was back in town, back from London, from Chelsea, where he lived, even then I'd felt little inclination to speak, to describe my thoughts and feelings, to complain about my students, my work.

Not that I'd hadn't things to say. I'd had plenty of things to say.

Certainly I had much on my mind when I rang Mary's doorbell that night. I'd spent the better part of the train ride from New Brunswick, then the taxi ride from Penn Station, mulling over the many things I wished to tell her before I left—none of which, as it turned out, I ever managed to say.

Once settled there beside her in their warm, familiar apartment, her boys in their pajamas, the television on, something within me gave way: I lost my conviction, my will. I felt ugly, peevish; my shirt, a favorite of mine, smelled sharply of sweat.

It occurred to me to gather my things and go, to tell her I wasn't feeling well, that I'd been sleeping poorly, that I'd text her as soon as I landed at Heathrow, but even that proved too much for me. In fact I felt queasy; my skin was clammy, my eyes were itchy and dry.

I was angry at Mary—obscurely, bitterly, so. And I was angry at myself. For months I'd been haunted by the impending trip, tormented by the thought of what I'd agreed to, by the sort of man I'd become. For all her gratitude, for all her efforts to reassure me, to mitigate the simple facts of the matter, I couldn't help feeling that, in having yielded to her inducements, her persuasion, I'd crossed a line over which I might never return. Indeed so monstrous was the thought of myself that night, so hideous, so loathsome, did I feel, that I'd have sprung to my feet and fled had not Ivan, the youngest of her boys, climbed into my lap. The simple gesture—the smell of his hair, the stars and planets on his pajamas—disarmed me. I couldn't move, I couldn't speak, but stared blindly at the television, listening in anguish to the thunder and rain.

Mary, perhaps to ease the tension between us, was speaking quickly, glibly, about her work, something she rarely did, scowling and laughing and sipping her wine.

She'd been struggling all day with the translation of a particular passage from Juan Goytisolo's mythoclastic novel, *Reivindicación del Conde Julián*, or *Count Julian*, as she'd decided to call it in English, the kitchen table covered with her papers and books. She told me she'd had a bad day of it—her headaches, the rain. She told me that Spanish was not the language I thought it was: it had everyone fooled.

I noticed that she'd painted her toenails; it was something she did when she was anxious, when she needed a distraction, some simple task with which to occupy her hands. She was still pretty. I felt it with a pang that night, and studied the small gold hoop in her ear, the slight, familiar curve of her nose. She hadn't worn makeup in years, so that her skin, while still taut, looked wan, almost ashen in the lamplight.

Behind her, on the wall between the windows, was a darkly framed ink painting called 'Crossing the River' by Yuan dynasty artist Shen Zongjing. For years I'd studied it from my place on the couch there—the waterfall, the cliffs, the tiny skiff bearing the scholar across the flood. Richard had bought it as a gift for her at a private auction in London. One New Year's Eve, when he'd had too much to drink, he'd forced me to stand before it, in the company of two women he knew, two colleagues from the university, as he'd described to us, in his bluff, assiduous way, some of its finer, more ethereal features, pointing first to the gnarled pine in the foreground, then to the lofty inscription in the upper righthand corner, then to the hints—mere intimations—of the mountains and ridgelines beyond. I remembered the restless sound of one of the women's bangles that night and the acrid-sweet scotch on his breath.

I hadn't seen Mary in months, since late December, when I'd accompanied her to Long Island, to Garden City, to visit her mother, Margaret, where she was still living, just a short walk from the bird sanctuary, in a modest house on Wickham Road. I'd always liked her mother, her frankness, her humor, her odd, unwonted interest in me. To my perennial surprise, she'd read everything I'd written over the years, no matter how recondite the subject, how specialized the language, how dry. She'd kept my books on a shelf beside her cookbooks in her bright yellow kitchen there, with its bright yellow air, so that whenever I'd visited we could talk.

On that bleak December day, just weeks before she'd died, we'd spoken at length about the book I'm writing now, a sociohistorical study of the French commemoration of the SS massacre at Oradour-sur-Glane, while Mary rummaged around in the drawers and closets upstairs. Her mother had enjoyed asking me about my trips there, to France, to the Limousin, where I'd spent weeks at a time, interviewing locals, young and old; combing through municipal archives, through heaps of old documents and photographs; and wandering wraith-like through the stark and crumbling ruins of the town—in search of what I still don't know. She'd loved to hear the way the locals spoke; she'd known some French and had marveled at their vernacular, their slang, though mostly what I'd shared with her were but excerpts from the many hours of transcripts I'd made, which I'd read aloud to her like scenes from a film script or play.

Mary herself had rarely joined us when we talked. She'd long been critical of my work, of my need to return, time and again, to Hitler and the Nazis and the horrors they'd wrought. I sensed that, deep down, she thought it dishonest of me, that I was trying to lay claim to a past, a trauma, that wasn't really mine. Of course, she'd never have said as much: that to be a Jew wasn't always enough.

I looked at her now, at her lips, her cheek, at the tiny, inkdrop birthmark by her ear. I knew she was miserable, that she'd been miserable for years. Long before she and Richard were married, she'd suspected him of having affairs, casual, mostly frivolous encounters that had seemed to pass quickly, like shadows, like rain. In time, for he'd confessed to nothing, she'd made an art of his deceptions, of their rhythms, their lights, of the strange and subtle charms they'd worked on his mind, so that over the years she'd sketched for me a veritable taxonomy of his moods and behaviors. The way he brushed his teeth, his hair, the way he laughed and sipped his coffee, even the way he shuddered briefly after pissing, seemed alive to her—appalling, minacious, obscene.

"Malraux was right," she'd declared to me one night, when Richard was away. She'd often called me late at night, when the boys were asleep, when she could no longer read or think and her brain beat dully like a small dark drum. Richard had been gone for weeks—in Belgium, I think— and had promised her he'd call. I remembered she'd seemed particularly distraught that evening, that the television or radio was on. And I remembered the catch in her voice when in her graceful, fateful French she'd declaimed: "'L'homme n'est pas ce qu'il pense être, il est ce qu'il cache.' Fucking brilliant, isn't it?" she'd cried. "We are what we conceal from others. *We are what we hide.*"

I remembered that. And I remembered the way I'd pictured her that night, as we'd talked on the phone. In my mind's eye I'd seen her standing at the tall glass doors in their living room, as the rain poured down upon the balcony outside, and upon the city, the streets, the boys asleep and dreaming in their beds down the hall, seen her standing there before the tall glass doors, looking out upon the narrow balcony where she liked to sit and smoke, an architectural aberration in the otherwise uniform design of the building that had made her gasp with pleasure when she'd first toured the apartment with Richard. She'd been charmed as a child by its fine, old-fashioned features: the high ceilings, transom windows, leafy crown moldings, and faded parquet floors. I'd imagined her standing there at the tall glass doors, as the rain beat down upon the rusted metal chairs, and upon the motley assortment of pots she'd collected over the years, with their crowns of blackened plants, seen her sipping her wine and gazing out over the darkened park below her at the lights of East Harlem and Queens.

She'd often stood that way; I'd seen it dozens of times before, the way she'd stood there at the tall glass doors, gazing down, over the cluttered balcony, at the dark, declivitous park, with its groves and pathways and drear outcroppings of rock, as if somehow it puzzled her, its contours, its scope, sometimes thinking or dreaming, sometimes startled by her likeness, her reflection, in the cold and rain-streaked glass.

I remembered the feeling I'd had that night, as I'd stood barefoot at the window in my kitchen, some thirty miles to the south, the sense that time—the succession of minutes, seasons, and years—had looped itself around us and paused, her voice an eddy of sorts, a respite, a surcease, a lull.

It had rained all day, a cold, stubborn rain, and I remembered looking out over the jumbled rooftops of the campus where I teach to the wide, dark swath of the Raritan River and the lights of Johnson Park. As I'd listened to Mary talking that night, to the steady, searching sound of her voice, I'd followed the homely little river in my mind, as it flowed eastward through the darkness to South Amboy, through Rocky Reach, Long Reach, Crab Island Reach, Red Root Reach, Keasby Reach, then into the bay, into the dawning, the sea. I'd pictured the bluefish and kingfish and muddy winter flounder with their millions of demersal eggs. I'd seen deep within the waters that night, seen tautogs and toadfish, seen silversides, killifish, and shrimp. And all around me I'd seen the shadows, the darkly twisting specters, of slender smoothhound sharks.

For I knew the waters well. Growing up, I'd spent many a long summer day with my stepfather, Bill, cruising the ragged coastline—the inlets, old oyster beds, and estuaries—in his trusty Boston Whaler. He was ex-Navy, a gruff, surly man with a blue glass eye who'd liked to fish, to fiddle with reels and baits, though we'd rarely caught a thing. On those hot, airless days, when the ocean lay about us like a sheet of mottled glass, we'd gone for hours without speaking, without so much as sighing or shifting our feet, when, as if touched by some fish-tailed spirit, he'd told me the things he knew.

Mary had talked that night as she'd talked to me before. She had a dogged, recursive way of speaking that always began with the same few subjects, in the same dark places. That night, as usual, it was of Richard whom she spoke— of his estrangement and deceit, of his refusal to acknowledge that other, furtive life of his, a life made vivid in her mind by the simple, glaring paucity of facts. For she knew little for certain, *for sure*. There were no photographs with which to indict him, no texts or phone calls, no lipstick on his collars or cheeks. When he dreamed beside her at night he snored lightly and never said a thing.

Richard puzzled her; he always had. He'd touch her cheek, stroke her hair; he had a tender, patient way of addressing her that often left her helpless and bleary with rage. For years, she'd been convinced he was leading a double life, a life parallel and indifferent to theirs, to the life he led with her and the boys, a betrayal, an *apostasy* (for such was her word for it), that over the years, had infected the very cells of her brain, so that everything she saw and felt was refracted through the prism of that dread, that knowledge, that pain.

Yet the worst part, she'd confessed to me, one damp summer morning, when we were resting on a bench in Morningside Park, where the boys had stopped to play, the part that frightened her most, was the possibility that he *knew* what he was doing to her, and had known it all along, that his behavior was not only deliberate but part and parcel of some larger, more sinister whole. He'd seemed to know precisely how much she could take, how hard he could push her, how far (in his absences, his indifference) he could go. After weeks of silence, of detachment, when he was scarcely home at all, the boys cranky, the kitchen filthy, the beds disheveled, unmade, just when she felt she couldn't bear another day of it, the futility, the despair, unwilling even to wash her hair or get dressed, it was always then that he'd surprise her, do something thought-ful, romantic, that he'd lead her like a princess to bed.

At such times, Richard had seemed almost unbear-ably himself again, kind and playful, alert as a suitor to her every interest and need. He'd risen early to make the coffee, something she herself had always done and looked forward to as a means of waking slowly, of taking the pulse of another listless day. She'd hardly known what to think of him when he was home. He'd fussed about the apart-ment all morning, folding laundry, paying bills, and help-ing the boys to tidy their rooms. Once, at an hour when he was usually gone, she'd found him seated at her desk before her laptop, his fingers resting lightly on the keys.

In such moods, he'd liked to ask her about her work, questions which, while always deftly, prudently posed, had never felt earnest, felt right. No matter how she'd replied to them, with what interest, what faith, in the end she'd always felt diminished by them, as if she'd known, somewhere deep inside herself, and for all her desire to *believe*, that he was only affecting an interest in her work, her thinking, that his questions were rarely anything more than show.

Yet such courtesies (for what else could she call them?) had done little to change the fact that he was often gone, and that when he was home he was rarely ever *home*. Once returned to New York, he spent the better part of his days squirreled away in his office behind the library, meeting with students, writing his lectures, and conferring with colleagues and experts in the field. It seemed to her he was always busy with someone or something, that he was always on his laptop or phone.

And then he was off again, to somewhere else—she'd lost track of the cities, the days.

"I think he's in Brussels now," she'd told me that night, the night she'd mentioned Malraux. "Though I can't be sure. He could be in Hong Kong instead. He likes it there, how crowded and lonely it is. He often says such things.

He likes me to think about them, which, naturally, *inevitably*, I do. He likes to plant them like tiny green seeds in my mind. It's a sort of a game he plays with me," she'd explained. "At first, I thought it malicious of him, sadistic really, as some of the seeds actually sprouted. And not all of them were flowers. Not by far.

"You see, for a time I'd convinced myself that he was not content simply to betray me, to betray our life together, our boys, but wanted—for some bleak, inexplicable reason—to break me down, bit by bit, until I was nothing but a jumble of parts on the floor. I'd often pictured it, you know, seen him standing above me with an arm of mine, with an ear, an eyeball, a leg. Such a curious feeling—like watching a mechanic or plumber at work!"

Once more she'd paused to sip her wine, I'd heard it, the sound, when to my relief she'd said, "Yet I no longer believe it. Not really. He's not that cunning, that cruel. You know him, Jacob; he's too vain, too impulsive, ever-distracted by some bright and shiny thing. No, I no longer believe he's doing it on purpose, to hurt me, that he's aware of it at all. I think it's simpler than that, more a quirk of his, a tic, something eccentric and reflexive over which he has little if any control.

"Which, of course, is not to absolve him of the responsibility for its effects," she'd insisted at once, as if to preclude a response from me. "He's a grown man, after all, one who's well aware of his talents, his charms. You've seen it yourself, the way he cuts a swath through a room. And then there are his students—good God, how they follow him about! Why, he's older than most of their fathers!"

Again I'd heard her sip her wine, followed by the stubborn striking of a match. "Yet none of that matters anymore," she'd declared wanly, taking a long, slow drag of her cigarette, when suddenly I'd heard over the phone the familiar cry of an ambulance on Amsterdam Avenue, which meant that, despite the cold, she'd opened one of the tall glass doors to the terrace to expel the smell of it, the smoke. "I mean, how can one hate a man for being so loved? It'd be like hating him for the color of his eyes or for the size of his feet." There'd come a pause, a pause so long I'd almost interjected, for I was tired and eager to sleep, when, in a weary, helpless tone, she'd added, "Yet hate him I do. With all my heart some days. The question is *why*? What crimes has he committed? What in fact has he done?"

I'd heard the questions before, many times, and had simply waited for her to answer them or dismiss them out of hand. "Certainly he's guilty," she'd averred forthwith, as if on cue. "At the very least *negligent*: he's often gone, is care-less with the boys, and thinks of nothing but his paintings and books. Then there's the fact that we almost never have sex anymore. It's true. I can hardly remember the last time he saw me naked. And there…there's the rub…"

"The rub?" I'd asked.

"You know the catch, the problem—it's all too obvious, too plain. It just doesn't feel right to me. It doesn't make sense. I mean, I blink, I screw up my eyes, and I still can't see the forest for the trees!"

At that point I remembered I'd heard a change in her voice, a shift in its timbre, its tone, that had put me on guard. "This jealousy," she'd said, at length, her voice abstracted, detached. "It's a curious thing, you know. It's like…it's like having termites in your house. For years they work away on you, gnawing patiently at the footings, at the headers and studs; you hardly know they're there. The only signs of them, of what they're doing, day after day, week after week, month after month, are the tiny piles of sawdust you find along the baseboards and in the backs of certain cupboards and drawers, which you vacuum up with hardly a thought as to what has made them, so that by the time you realize what's happened it's too late: the house collapses one night while you sleep."

There'd come another stretch of silence, I'd heard her close the door, when, with a catch in her voice, she'd pleaded, "Don't you see, Jacob? I'm sick of it. I'm sick of thinking about him, about where he goes and who he meets with and what they talk about, if they talk about me. I can't take it anymore. I *can't*. Something—surely *something*—has to give!"

She'd seemed particularly desperate that night; surely something was different, had changed, and in a flash I'd pictured her slitting her wrists or swallowing a bottle of pills. I knew that she'd recently terminated her relationship with her latest therapist after he'd suggested to her, perhaps in a careless moment, that her suspicions, her anger, might be rooted in envy, in her envy of Richard's career. She'd raged for days about the remark, about the inability of men to see beyond the limits of their egos, their pricks, when she'd taken aim at herself, reproving herself so harshly, with such bitter precision, I'd been forced to intervene.

When next she'd spoken (I'd heard the clink of her glass in the sink), she'd sounded sullen, defeated, spent, as if at last she'd depleted some vast inner store of feeling and was finally ready to sleep. "My mother...my mother used to wrinkle her nose at me whenever I complained about Richard. She'd have none of it, you see. For all her doilies and biscuits and tea, she was a fatalist at heart. She believed that life—whatever we hoped of it—always did its own damned thing!" I'd heard her laugh, a deep, sullen laugh, when she'd conceded, "She was wise in her way, my mother. I can see that now. She knew what such anguish could do.

"And that's the point," she'd remarked, just when I'd thought she was about to hang up. "I'm tired of being suspicious, of worrying about Richard, of trying to figure him out. I mean, what if he's not that interesting? What if he's not that complex? It's occurred to me, you know. What if all the stories I've been telling myself about him are just that—*stories*, only fictions in my head?"

It too was a tack I'd heard before and was about to interrupt her, to say goodnight, when again she'd surprised me. "I'm serious, Jacob. Lately things have changed between us. It's different somehow. *He's* different."

"Different? Different how?" I'd said.

"I'm not sure. It's like…It's like, even when I'm looking right at him, I have trouble actually *seeing* him. He seems to ripple and pulse before me, as if his entire being is in flux. You know, like a mirage in the desert, like the flickering of a bulb before it goes dark.

"I know it sounds crazy, but what if all along I've been wrong about him? Think about it. What if the man I fell in love with has never really existed? What if all this time, Richard—the *real* Richard—has been leading a quiet, blameless life right here beside me, and all without the slightest intention of deceiving me, of breaking my heart? Is it possible that I've been living with a stranger after all, a figment of my own most-desperate making?"

At that she'd stopped abruptly, seemingly aghast at the implications of what she'd said. I'd heard her mumble something, something about the rain, about the dryness of her skin, when in the same remote, discarnate voice she'd said, "It's funny. I remember, when my mother died, being struck by how little there was to think about when I thought about her. I was riding the train to Garden City to finish sorting her things, it was raining like today, and all I could remember about her was the smell of her house and the ugly bunion on her toe. Somehow that was it. There was nothing more. There was nowhere else for my mind to go!"

"But, Mary, you were grieving!" I'd chided her, impatiently. "It happens to everyone. One's mind, one's memory, goes blank."

"Yes, but that wasn't it," she'd countered at once, as if quickened by my response. "It wasn't grief, I tell you, I'm certain of it, for even weeks later I couldn't remember anything more than that smell and that ugly old bunion on her toe! Surely there was more to my mother than that…"

"Of course there was! You know there was. But what does any of it have to do with Richard? The case of your mother seems entirely different."

"Well, it's not!" she'd insisted, coldly. "I mean, Richard, my mother…what if all along I've been deluding myself about them, about everyone—about you? That's what frightens me. What if the problem, the culprit, is *me*?"

"Come on, Mary. You don't honestly believe that, that you've simply imagined it all."

"Believe it?" she'd cried. "Sometimes it's all I've got! For God's sake, Jacob, can't you see what he's done?"

Ivan, feeling restless, had returned to his place on the floor beside his brother, and I tried now to focus on what Mary was telling me about her work that day, something about Goytisolo's language, about its violence and fragmentation, but was distracted by the rain and thunder, and by the manic flashing of the television. Clearly she was uncomfortable, and I was thinking of something to say, something to break the spell of her talking, when her cell phone buzzed—another text from her sister, no doubt, her sister, Grace, with whom, until lately, she'd never been close.

I watched her for a moment, as she tapped away at the tiny keys, then rose to the tall glass doors to consider the pale night sky. Loathe as I was to admit it, I was looking forward to the trip, to getting away for a while. I'd finished packing that morning. I'd stopped my mail, cleaned the bathroom, and had gotten rid of everything perishable in the refrigerator. All that remained to be done was to leave a message for my neighbor, a colleague from Lagos, who'd agreed to feed my cat, a one-eyed Siamese named Max.

With a rush of pleasure now, I pictured the patchwork fields of Oxfordshire, the rolling hills, then Oxford itself, as one approached it by train—the meadows and churches, the colleges and gardens, the sluggish old Thames, as it wound its way through the ancient, cloistered city.

I was thinking of a pub there, where I used to go for lunch, when I realized that Mary had finished texting and was staring at me, head cocked, as she did when she felt I was being fractious. I heard her sniffle, then sigh, only to remark, as if merely taking up the thread of an earlier conversation, "You've been there before." I thought it a curious way of starting—half-apology, half-rejoinder. "I mean, you know your way around. You said so yourself."

I resisted looking at her, for I was unwilling to concede the point. At least yet. Instead I peered out the window, taking a long, slow sip of my wine.

"Jacob, you told me you were fond of it. You did!"

It was true. I cherished the time I'd spent there in Oxford. It was there I'd fallen in love.

Still, I refused to reply to her, to give her the satisfaction, and was thinking of bidding her goodbye, of making my way home again, after all I had to be up early, when she cried, "That woman! What was the name of that woman you met there? You know. She was Scottish, I think. From Glasgow or Aberdeen."

"Cardiff," I corrected her.

"Cardiff?"

"The city she was from." I was going to leave it at that, when I added, "Her name, by the way, was Celeste."

"Celeste—that's right!" cried Mary, clearly pleased to have gotten me talking. I, however, was in no mood to speak further and patted my pockets, as if feeling for my cell phone, my keys. "So she was Welsh?" she pressed me, surprised. "How strange! I could have sworn she was Scottish, what with that hair and those freckles. You showed me a photograph, remember? I called her your Lorna Doone!" At that she poked me in the ribs. "Come on, Jacob," she insisted with impatience. "You know what this means to me. You're the only person I trust."

I was about to speak, I felt the anger rising in me, when in a dark and level voice she said, "You…you of all people, you *know* what I've been through. The price I've paid. And for what? For this?" she scoffed, gesturing vaguely about her, at the books and vases, at the prints and paintings on the walls. "Time after time he does this to us. The boys wait, they cry, he doesn't call. Even when he returns he doesn't say a thing. Just musses their hair and grins. No apology. *Nothing.* And then he's too busy for them, for me. He's got his meetings and his classes. He's got another deadline for his book.

"Don't you see? I'm trapped, I'm drowning. I think I'm losing my mind." She raised her wine glass to her lips, then set it down again. "Just this morning…just this morning I thought I heard my mother talking to me from the kitchen. I was in the bathroom getting dressed when I distinctly heard her voice, heard her call out to me, you know that voice of hers, something about coffee or tea." Weary, trembling, she grimaced. "And that's nothing. The real stuff happens late at night, when the boys are asleep and there's nothing I can do!"

Briefly she held her head in her hands. When she looked at me her cheeks were streaked with tears. "Honestly, I'm a mess, a disaster. Even my own brother can't bear to spend time with me anymore. Tell me, Jacob, what's the matter with me? I think they're something wrong with my brain."

I watched her swallow the last of her wine, then wipe her mouth with the back of her hand. Shaking her head, she said, "Of course, Grace…she's never liked Richard, never trusted him. She says I should just divorce the bastard, change the locks on the door. She finds me pathetic, you know. Says I've got no courage, no pride. She told me that, just now, or reminded me of it, anyway, for she's said it to me before. She often says such things, that I'm dull and spineless, that if in fact I hate Richard, as I claim, I hate myself much more. In the end, she says, it's always about shame and self-loathing, that she detests my puppet-face."

"Your puppet-face?"

"Yes, she says she's watched me for years, the way I dance for Richard like a puppet on strings." She bristled at the thought of it, when she said, "Of course she's a bitch, my sister. You've met her. With that hair, those nails. She thinks she knows it all, that she understands my marriage, my life. She's a Catholic, after all: Christ this, Christ that. Mother Mary, Mistress of God. I remember her telling me, the night of my wedding, that I'd rue the day I met him. And I remember how I'd laughed in her face!"

The television program had just ended, the boys began to stir, and Mary was about to whisk them off to bed, when she said, "The fact is, she's right about me. She's often so *terribly* right."

Left alone, I did what I always do: I wandered around the handsome room, touching this, examining that, and making an inventory of the various books and paintings and prints. Richard was a collector of things, of things

Chinese—porcelain and jade, amulets and coins, and of fine old ink paintings on paper and silk, especially those of the 'literati' or poet-painters of the Yuan and Ming dynasties. What little I knew of the pieces I knew from him, from his often lively descriptions of them.

Years ago, he'd found in me a ready, if somewhat impercipient pupil. He liked to drink, and when he drank he liked to talk about his work: about Presence and Absence; about Wang Ch'ung, Su Shih, and Chuang-tsu; and about the ancient Chinese system of appraising art, of *shen*, *miao*, *neng*, and *yi*.

One of his favorite games was to have me choose three artifacts in the apartment at random—no matter the period or dynasty, no matter the medium, material, or style—and set them before him on the kitchen table. For a moment, he'd blink his eyes and sigh, he'd groan and sputter, like a child he'd squeeze his eyes shut, when with a sudden exhalation he'd *speak*, weaving the items together in a narrative so fine, so seemly, that at times I'd actually gasped.

I heard one of the boys scream from down the hallway, then Mary's plaintive voice.

Upon a sip of wine, I picked up a piece I knew well, a small celadon bowl from the Song dynasty with a finely crackled olive-green glaze. While not particularly valuable—it was one of untold dozens of its kind—there was something I liked about it. It was coarse to the touch and marred, here and there, by reddish-brown patches, which, as Richard had explained to me one night, were the result of either inexpert or improper firing, of too much or too little heat. Reflexively I sniffed the bowl, turned it round in my hands, then set it back in its stand on the shelf.

The wine had blurred the edges of my mood, so that mostly what I felt was a pleasant confusion, a pale and gauzy relief.

It was still raining outside and I stood for a moment in the old butler's pantry, admiring Richard's collection of Chinese brush pots. Typically made of porcelain, ivory, jade, or horn, and often decorated with traditional symbols and motifs, such pots were at one time to be found, along with a variety of inkstones and brushes, on every scholar's desk. I thought about opening the case, I liked to handle them, but was distracted by the sound of Mary's voice as she read aloud to the boys in their room down the hall.

As usual, when Richard was away, I couldn't resist having a look at his study, a dark, pantry-like room just off the kitchen, with its squat wooden desk, cracked leather armchair, and discrepantly large reproduction of one of

Warhol's garish Maos. Books were scattered everywhere—perhaps he'd been looking for one before he left—so that I had to make my way through the dimly lit room with care.

I liked to sit in Richard's chair when he was gone, to consider what he was reading and to listen to the sounds of the city from there. The only window in the room opened onto a narrow air shaft, its panes all but occluded by pigeon dung and soot. The room itself smelled stale, and faintly of tobacco, though he hadn't smoked a pipe in years.

Resisting the urge to sit now, I perused the books on his shelves, most of them in Chinese, German, and French, though there were plenty in English, too, not a few of which he'd shown me before: *Hunger Mountain*; *Principles of Chinese Painting*; *300 Tang Poems*; *Empty and Full*; *Classical Chinese Medicine*; *Hills Beyond a River*; *Shitao (1642-1707): The Savior of the World*; *The Songs of Chu*; *The Peach Blossom Fan*; *Three Alternative Histories of Chinese Painting*; *Wild Geese Returning*; and, bristling with colored tabs on the little brass table by his chair, a tattered paperback called *The Chinese on the Art of Painting* translated and annotated by a Swede named Osvald Sirén.

Propped against the spines of some of his books were a number of framed and unframed photographs, some of which were of Mary, of Mary and the boys, though most of which had been taken long before he'd met her, when he'd lived as a student in Taiwan.

He'd often spoken to me of his time there, in Taipei, sparkling, largely halcyon days when he'd studied hard, eaten well, and spent the weekends either hiking in the mountains or bathing alone at one of the popular nearby beaches. He'd told me once, when we were looking at a small, framed photograph he kept by his chair, one of him in sunglasses with a grinning young friend named Shu-chen, that it surprised him, some days, that he'd ever come back.

On his desk by the lamp I found the familiar jade carving of a goldfish from the Qianlong period of the Qing dynasty. It was a simple, elegant piece, cool and dappled and surprisingly light to the touch. While talking he'd often fondled it, as if as a fetish, a dream.

There too was a draft of the first two chapters of his latest book, a conceptual study of Taoist and Ch'an spirituality through the lens of a single painting by the monk and artist, Shih T'ao. While Richard had mentioned the project, indeed had shown me a copy of the painting itself, the book's title—*Existence: A Story*—was new to me. I thought it brazen, outrageous, *sublime*, and was thumbing quickly through the freshly printed pages, when I heard Mary in the kitchen.

"You know what they say about curiosity, don't you?" she chided me, the moment I appeared. For some reason she'd put on lipstick.

"Why the lipstick?" I asked.

"I don't know, really. I ordered it a while ago. I guess I wanted to know what you think."

"I think it's pretty," I said.

She feigned a smile, shrugged her shoulders. "So what did you find in there?"

"In there? Nothing to speak of. No clues, if that's what you mean."

"I don't *mean* anything," she scoffed, wearily. "It seems I rarely mean anything anymore."

She was staring listlessly into the refrigerator. In its light I could see the tracery of fine blue veins in her neck. I thought she might stand there all night, I couldn't move, I couldn't breathe, when all at once she said, "Some days it just feels like everyone is lying to me—the custodian; the guy at the deli; the woman, Alyssa, who cuts my hair. Even the boys… The other day Jack lied to my face about some silly little toy he'd broken. I know he's a child, that children lie, but still I wept. I couldn't help it, I cried and cried and cried."

Eager to distract her, to speak of something else, I said, "Richard's new book…has he told you much about it?"

"No, not much," she muttered, selecting a nearly empty jar of pickles before returning it to the shelf. "He said he'd left me some chapters to read. I just haven't had the time."

In the past, she'd taken a special interest in his work, traveling with him to China, Singapore, and Taiwan, examining the various paintings that concerned him, and proofreading his drafts and galleys—a fact for which he'd credited her at the back of every book.

Yet those days were gone.

I said, "It was nice to see the boys tonight. You know, Ivan's got your ears."

"My ears!" she snapped, aghast. "You must be joking! Why, he's the spitting image of his father. The ears, the eyes, the mouth. You should see the way he looks at me some days—the resentment, the disgust! Once he starts a sulk he can ignore me for days."

My head ached, I was impatient to go, but felt the need to say something—anything to lighten the mood. "Do you remember that summer we took the boys to the zoo?" Feeling restless one day we'd taken the train to the Bronx.

"Yes, it was fun, wasn't it?" she said, turning slowly to look at me, only to exclaim, "And the rain! Do you remember the rain?"

"Yes, we got soaked to the skin! I remember the boys had loved the poison frogs."

Mary had closed the refrigerator and, toying with a matchbook, was contemplating a cigarette, a habit she'd been trying to break, when I led her out into the foyer.

"So you have your tickets?' she asked uneasily, as I shrugged on my jacket. It was odd: now that the time had come for me to speak, I had nothing to say.

"Well, it's all in here," she said, handing me the folder she'd prepared for me. "As I said, I've booked you a room at the Vanbrugh Hotel. Do you know it? It's small and quiet and gets some excellent reviews. I thought you'd like to be right there in town."

She'd unbolted the door without opening it, so that there was an awkward moment between us, when abruptly, as if she'd been holding her breath, she exclaimed, "Of course I'll reimburse you, Jacob. For everything I can!"

THE TRENTON-BOUND TRAIN WAS UNUSUALLY crowded at that hour. On such an inclement night, I'd expected to find most of the cars empty.

Once seated by a window, across from a young man on crutches and an elderly woman with her knitting, I took out the book I'd been reading, a short novel by the Spanish writer Ana María Matute called *Primera memoria*. Mary had given me a copy of it for my birthday one year, but I'd never gotten around to reading it.

As usual I considered the cover—a graphically spare, graphically pleasing depiction of a patch of pale blue ocean, a yellow sky with an orange sun, and a young woman peering out at the world through an aperture on the horizon line, as if the sea and sky had been folded back. I scanned the plaudits on the opening pages, rereading one by a Spanish author named Milena Busquets, which I'd liked, then another, a longer, more effusive one, by the Peruvian writer, Mario Vargas Llosa, before turning to the page I'd marked with a business card from Hôtel des Deux Avenues, the small hotel, near the Arc de Triomphe, in which I'd stayed with Mary one fall.

I was at a part in the story in which the orphaned teen-aged narrator, Matia, a girl adrift in her grandmother's house on the island of Mallorca, during the Spanish Civil War, was in her Aunt Emilia's room with her, watching the cowed and helpless woman, with her 'great belly and breasts', as she poured herself a brandy from a bottle she kept hidden in the wardrobe into a ruby-red glass. Matia watched her with a torpid fascination as she gulped down the liquor, lighted a cigarette, then slumped down in an old armchair by the window to look at some magazines, when, without warning, she, Matia, was struck by the horror of it all: *Suddenly there was something strange in the room, as if someone had brought in the whips and harnesses from the patio and hung them on the wall. Something brutal and cruel came and tore in two the stillness of Aunt Emilia's room...*

The train was just pulling into the station in Newark when I looked up from my reading. It seemed the rain had finally stopped.

I was tired, I felt an unusual exhaustion in my bones, and briefly closed my eyes. I was pleased to have finally begun the novel, though I had a host of other, more pressing things to read, and thought briefly of the ways I'd praise it to Mary, when I returned from England. It was no wonder she admired it—the language, the setting, the remote, if still-virulent war.

Years before, she'd written her dissertation on the author, on the various archetypes to be found in her work. Yet in the end it had been the craft of translation that had most appealed to her. Shortly after she'd earned her degree, she'd compiled a prize-winning anthology of the work of Republican poets living in exile in Paris during the Spanish Civil War, a work that had distinguished her in certain academic circles, both here and abroad.

Following her success, after a year or more of lecturing, attending conferences, and sitting for interviews, she'd turned her thoughts and eyes elsewhere, away from Europe, from Spain, exploring the work of mostly lesser-known female poets from Mexico and Nicaragua, from Colombia, Chile, and Argentina, from Uruguay, Paraguay, and Peru.

And now? For months now, she'd been toiling away on her translation of the novel, *Reivindicación del Conde Julián* by the Spaniard, Juan Goytisolo, the second in his famous Álvaro Mendiola trilogy, an undertaking so trying, so ambitious, it had all but overwhelmed her.

The train shuddered on its tracks and for a while

I gazed out the rain-streaked window, distracted by thoughts of my flight the next day and by the deep, heavy darkness of the world, which lay in patches, in pools.

It had rained nearly every day that Mary and I were in Paris, when she was laying the groundwork for her current project, then still a pipedream—a happy, three-week sojourn of eating, drinking, and wandering wet and exhilarated through the lonely, church-like spaces of libraries, galleries, and museums. We'd made an adventure of it, while there together, browsing bookshops, meeting with writers and scholars, and tracking the ghost of the captious Goytosilo through the rainy, windswept streets.

Together, we'd followed him everywhere that fall—to the apartment where he'd lived with his wife on rue Poissonnière, to the offices of Gallimard, in which briefly he'd worked as a reader, to the cafés of Montparnasse and Saint-Germain-des-Prés, where he'd gathered weekly with his friends and fellow-antifascists: Marguerite Duras, Roland Barthes, Maurice Blanchot, and the vagabond saint, Jean Genet, as well as with such Republicans and compatriots as he could still find there, in Paris, men and women like Alfonso Sastre, Eva Forest, Luis Buñuel, Ricardo Muñoz Suay, Tuñón de Lara, and the factionary Antonio Soriano, owner of the popular Spanish bookshop on nearby rue de Seine.

Mary had seemed younger on that trip, bolder, more capricious, more akin to the woman I'd known. Every day we'd met for breakfast in the grotto-like basement of the hotel, with its half a dozen tables and its ample selection of fruits, cereals, yogurts, and croissants. It was she who'd chosen the place, attracted by its modesty and price, and by its location, just a short walk from Parc Monceau.

Some mornings, when we'd met in the basement for breakfast, she'd been eager to talk with me, to sketch out the day before us. She'd liked to consult her various guidebooks and maps of the city, which she'd scored with an assortment of oddly colored pens. It was there, too, some days, when the weather was particularly grim, that she'd begged me to continue south with her, after Paris, to Barcelona, where Goytisolo was born, then south again to Morocco, to Tangier, to where he'd fled, once a widower, once an openly gay man, ending finally in the Almoravid capital of Marrakesh, in which ancient red-walled city the apostate-decrier had lived until his death, whiling away the hours each day at the popular Café de France, perched high above the Djemaa el-Fna.

Then, too, there were mornings when she'd scarcely said a thing to me, sipping her coffee, checking the texts and messages on her phone, and riffling impatiently through the pages of *Le Monde*.

She'd rarely mentioned Richard on the trip, at least not by name. Instead she'd talked her way around him, an evasion, a circumlocution, I'd found baffling, pointless, almost superstitiously strange.

She'd walked with a fury that fall. Every day we'd set out early, sometimes with a particular place in mind, some gallery, archive, or patisserie, though mostly we'd simply wandered our way through the grave, immutable city, marveling like children at the way it had unfolded itself before us—street by street, block by block, mood by wistful mood.

At times, as we'd walked, Mary had hooked her arm through mine, she'd teased me, she'd kissed me on my cheeks, the nose. Once in Montmartre, on the steps of Sacré Coeur, she'd told me she loved me in a way she'd never loved anyone else. And I remember how suddenly physical I'd felt there, amidst the pilgrims like me, how fleshly and earthly and *real*.

Yet the feeling hadn't lasted. How could it have? By the time we'd returned to the hotel, she'd turned inward again, away from me, her eyes occluded, self-seeking, so that I'd drifted up the stairs behind her, as abject, as insubstantial, as a whisper, a ghost.

On a whim one morning, when the wind had died out and the clouds were only threatening rain, we'd taken the metro to Buttes-Chaumont Park, in the northeast of Paris, to see Le temple de la Sybille, an architectural folly perched high above the lake there, for no other reason than that Goytisolo had once mentioned it in a letter to a friend.

We'd entered the park, just steps from the busy metro station, by a narrow iron gate from which we'd followed a trail through a tangle of naked trees and shrubs to an open space of diverging cinder paths with their vernacular green benches, from where we'd made our way along a wider route called L'Avenue de la Cascade that had led us away from the busy rue Botzaris on one side, and the rue de Crimée on the other, toward the heart of the park itself—the modest lake in which, upon a bluff of gypsum and limestone, stood the curious Temple of the Sybille.

I remembered being struck by the park's terrain, so variable, uneven, so at odds with the other parks I knew, a landscape that had seemed as lush and mysterious as the jungles of Bali or the gorges and pillars of Wulingyuan, an impression confirmed at once by Mary who'd explained to me, with the aid of one of her guidebooks, that the park, now so verdant, so coy, had been built upon the remains of an old quarry, the earth beneath our feet as riddled with holes and hollows as a wheel of Swiss cheese. The park, which took its name from the older Chauve-mont or 'bare hill', had long been a wasteland of sorts, a barren tract of land that had served successively as a garbage dump, a depository for sewage, an abattoir for horses, and a site—known as the Gibbet of Montfaucon—for the exhibition of recently executed criminals.

To reach the island and the Temple that crowned its bluff we'd had to cross a footbridge over murky green water, then climb a path that rose steeply to the top. The view from there, from within the folly itself, had proven even finer, more rewarding than we'd expected, so that for a time we'd stood there without speaking, gazing out over the pale, unvanquished city, adrift and alone in our per-mutable selves.

It was there, within the Roman-style folly, then densely tagged with graffiti, that Mary had told me about her dream. It was a dream she'd had before, many times, starting when she was young, if with disturbing varia-tions, so that she'd wondered, at points, if in fact it was the same dream at all or just a series of separate, interlocking dreams, the edges or orbits of which occasionally over-lapped.

In the dream she was never herself, at least not phys-ically, but rather a clear, floating, sometimes amniotic, sometimes gelatinous amalgam of the thoughts and feel-ings of others, of the people she knew and loved, as well as of those of perfect strangers, of people who'd seen her on the bus or the subway or had passed her by chance in the street.

Always in the dream she felt helpless, indefinite, yet strangely, darkly supreme. It was not a power she felt, as such, a power over others, over things, but more of an impulse, an animus, that seemed to exist within itself and for itself, an easy, self-sufficient force that swirled within and about her with a bright, if guttering light.

She'd spoken slowly, impassively that day, where we'd stood huddled together in the folly on the bluff, as if even then in a trance, a dream, so that I'd been able to study her features, as she spoke—her lips, her hair, her pale and bloodless cheeks—beneath the whole of which there'd seemed to flicker a troupe of other persons, of souls.

I was thinking of that outing, of Mary's dream, the book still open in my lap, when I recalled the curious term I'd seen that evening in the pages on Richard's desk. *Existence-tissue*. It seemed an odd, even clumsy translation for such a deft and eloquent writer as Richard. To what exactly did it refer?

Again, the train began to slow down and I watched the young man with crutches as he struggled to his feet, slipped his backpack over his shoulders, and made his way down the aisle in a way that struck me as familiar, significant, though I couldn't say how.

The city of Elizabeth was the next stop on the line, then Linden, Rahway, and Metro Park. From there it would be just minutes to New Brunswick.

It was raining lightly when I left the station and made the short walk back to my apartment at the edge of the deserted campus. Once inside I hung up my coat behind the door, but resisted the urge to turn on the lights. Instead I felt my way through the sparsely furnished room to my desk in the corner by the window. From there I could see the paths and pavilions of Johnson Park.

My head ached from the wine, I felt a tension in my jaw, and thought briefly of taking some aspirin, but hadn't the will, the volition, to move. Someone nearby was playing music; it sounded like Mozart, like the overture to *Don Giovanni*, but I couldn't be sure. I heard the flushing of the toilet in the apartment directly above me, followed by the angry rattle of pipes, then what sounded like Haydn instead.

My flight tomorrow was scheduled to depart from Newark at 9:40 a.m. and, after a quick recalculation of the time, I set the alarm on my phone.

I was restless and considered doing a little work to settle my mind before sleeping. My editor had made a few suggestions about the opening chapter of my book and I was eager to attend to them, at least to get a better sense of her meaning.

Flipping on the desk lamp, I was struck by the warm, familiar glow it cast over everything assembled there, and for a moment I simply admired it all—the photographs, my thesaurus and pens, the brightly painted statue of Ganesh. The student who'd given it to me, a boy named Nikhil, had died one day of some mysterious cause, not long after completing my class.

I opened up my laptop, then briefly examined the books I'd set aside to take with me to Oxford, which I'd arranged, along with a number of colored binders, on a corner of my desk.

It was my plan, while away, to revise the fourth and thematically pivotal chapter of my book. Called 'The Memorial Landscape', it was really the heart of my argument, my thesis, describing, as it did, the complex, if largely fanciful role of the massacre at Oradour-sur-Glane in France's national reckoning with the German occupation, with its own still-festering wounds.

It seemed a reasonable expectation. After all, I'd only agreed to *watch* Richard, while in Oxford, to see what he did each day and take notes. I had no intention of interacting with him.

It wasn't that I didn't enjoy his company. I did. In fact I marveled at his zeal for life, at his seemingly endless enthusiasms. Above all, I marveled at the curious power he possessed of making one feel connected, consistent, and whole. I'd long thought (and had often teased him about it) that he'd have made a worthy Ch'an master.

Ever since we'd met, shortly after he and Mary had started dating, he'd treated me with a warmth and affection which I'd often been at a loss to reciprocate. He'd seemed to like me, my work, my company, and had made a point of including me in their lives, so that for years, before I'd left the city, the three of us had been inseparable.

Again I thought of the book he was writing, of its title, *Existence*, and wondered—with a touch of reproof—at his audacity, his pluck.

I myself had never been bold enough, always taking the path of least resistance, aiming always for what was well within my reach. I'd long felt that, whatever my reasons for it (and I could think of many), I'd always restrained myself, I'd always held back. Even the book I was writing now seemed to me a tepid, half-hearted affair, when compared to the least of Richard's work.

That morning, I'd printed out the first five chapters and scanned them now with a rising dismay, so that once in bed I couldn't sleep. At first the room seemed too cold, then too airless, too hot.

Not for the first time I wondered what it was all about— my research and writing, my lonely, often bewildering trips to France, to the Limousin, to meet with the locals there, elders mostly, who said little, smiled wryly, and often plied me for money and drinks. My research and writing—what was it all about? What was I after? What if anything did I hope to find?

It was a perplexity I'd felt before, at least once particularly, when I was a student in graduate school. A friend and fellow classmate of mine had given me a copy of 'The Retreat from the Word' an essay by philosopher and literary critic, George Steiner. But a single reading of it had been enough to stagger me, to leave me reeling for days. Even now I could feel its sting.

'The Apostle tells us that in the beginning was the Word,' Steiner had begun. 'He gives us no assurance as to the end.' From there, with a force of rhetoric I'd been helpless to contest, he'd described what he called *la crise du langage*, the now-widespread belief that language itself had failed us as human beings, that as a means, a medium, it was no longer 'commensurate with the manifold truths of the experienced world.'

It was to mathematics and science, he'd claimed, to the material conditions of existence, that the world had turned its anxious eyes, disciplines which, in a matter of decades, had extended their reach into every realm of life, infusing even the most commonplace thinking and gestures with what he'd called 'the cult of the positive, the exact, and the predicative.'

I couldn't remember how long I'd sat there in my room with the essay in my lap, what thoughts I'd had, what feelings. All I remembered was a sense of emptiness, of dissipation, an inkling (I'd heard the traffic on the avenue) that everything and nothing was real.

Once I'd tried to explain it to Mary's mother. She'd asked me why I'd never married, and I'd tried to describe for her the futility I felt some days, the sudden, plangent sense of my own absurdity that made it hard just to get out of bed.

Kicking off the sheet now, I switched on the light, turned on the fan, and retrieved my laptop from my desk. There were two new emails from a colleague of mine, a reminder from the airline, and a short essay by my brother-in-law, David, about a dragonfly he'd been studying called the Common Green Darner.

The last time I'd seen him, more than a year ago, I'd asked him about his work, there in the wetlands of Maine, and he'd promised to send me a draft of an essay he was writing for a local wildlife consortium as soon it was done. The opening was diverting, delightful:

Following a long winter and the first fickle

days of spring, Maine naturalists await their favorite harbinger of the coming growing season. Along with swelling tree buds, migrant swallows, trillium blossoms, and clucking wood frogs, the longer days bring some of our earliest winged insects, including spring azure butterflies, newly emerged bumble bee queens, and one of my favorites, a dragonfly with the prosaic name, Common Green Darner, *Anax junius* to scientists. Maine's wetlands are an especially productive place to monitor for early signs of insect activity. Indeed, when scanning the marshy shoreline below my Kennebec County home on a warm day in late April, I am often rewarded by the first appearance of the Green Darner patrolling over last season's brown and weathered cattails. But where did this lively creature come from, and where is it going?

In fact I was so charmed by the essay that I wrote to David at once to tell him. I was tempted to send a quick note to my sister, as well, to say hello and to ask about the kids, but decided against it. We'd barely spoken in recent years—the result of an argument about our father, about his drinking and medications, the facts of which were now hopelessly muddled in my brain.

Returning my laptop to my desk, I got back into bed and switched off the light. The Common Green Darner.

I felt better for having read the essay, and for a time I amused myself with thoughts of cattails and dragonflies and grumbling bumble bee queens. Yet it wasn't long before my affliction returned. I thought of the book I was writing—of de Gaulle and Petain, of the Comité du Souvenir, of the insufficiency, the *failure*, of words.

For a period, following my move to New Brunswick, I'd been proud of my life here alone. I'd traveled, I'd focused on my teaching and writing—and all with some pleasing results. I'd walked everywhere in the modest city, had eaten at restaurants with a book or laptop in hand, and had thought nothing of reserving a room in a hotel somewhere, when I'd felt the need to get away. And over time I'd grown accustomed to my mind and its ways, to the gentle, anxious thrumming of my heart.

Yet it wasn't long before I'd grown sullen and restless. Within a year of beginning my new job, I'd felt I'd exhausted my resources here. The city was ugly, neglected. I'd stopped going out, had swallowed my dinner in front of the television, and had begun to resent my students for their boorish self-assertion and impatience with difficult things. My colleagues too, at first so lively, so engaging, suddenly had seemed dull to me—at once specious, grudging, and vain. I'd avoided them at work and had declined their occasional invitations, unwilling anymore to hear them talk about their children, their vacations, their pets. More than anything, I'd longed to return to New York, to Manhattan, and had wondered almost daily—with what at times had seemed a hysterical confusion—why in the world I'd left.

Initially, I'd lost touch with Mary. I'd been so busy with my teaching and writing, and with my trips to France, that I'd hardly considered her, or our relationship, except perhaps vaguely, when suddenly, like a flash of lightning, just the thought of her, of our late-night dinners together, of our walks together in Morningside Park, had been enough to cripple me for days.

The first time it had happened I was at a party at a colleague's house. Drinks had been served, it was snowing outside. I remember I was sipping a bourbon by the window in the den, there was chatter all around me, when I was struck by a wave of sadness that nearly knocked me off my feet. I pictured Mary, her eyes, the curve of her neck, and nearly choked on my longing, my grief. I was in love with her—so much was plain. I'd always been in love with her, though I'd cloaked it in other things. I'd left New York for no other reason than to get away from her. I could admit that now, that I'd cut off my nose to spite my face.

The night she'd asked me to go to England for her I'd practically cried with relief. Babbling, elated, I'd agreed to her request at once, indeed too quickly, for she'd laughed at me, at my reckless consent, so that my cheeks had burned with shame.

It was only many days later that I'd allowed myself to consider her request in earnest, to appraise it more objectively, if with a lingering sense of chagrin. She was asking me to spy on her husband, my colleague and friend, to trail him through the streets of Oxford and record what he did. She was asking me to betray him, to betray *myself*—and all because she herself felt betrayed.

I'd thought hard about refusing her; indeed I'd rehearsed what I'd say—that she was bitter and angry, that she was selfish, neurotic, and cruel. I was a grown man, after all, not some boy, some minion, ever-poised to do her bidding. I could have said all of that, I could have said no. Yet I hadn't; I hadn't said a thing. Instead I'd simply ignored her, refusing to respond to her texts and calls. Still smarting from her words, I'd done my best not to think of her at all.

I was coming out of class one day, a student on either side of me, when I'd nearly collided with her, where she was standing in the hallway.

"Mary!" I'd cried, doing my best to master my expression, for the sight of her had triggered a host of murky feelings in me. "What are you doing here?"

"I've come to take you to dinner!" she'd replied simply, seizing me by the arm. "You're angry at me, I know. You have every right to be. Just give me a chance to explain."

We'd talked for hours that night, first in the restaurant, then back at my apartment, which she'd never seen before nor ever even asked about.

She'd spoken of many things that evening—of her career, her dreams; of Richard and the boys; of the time, not long after college, when, after a night of watching fireworks from a rooftop in Brooklyn, we'd returned to my place and had sex.

She'd remembered the night (I was sure she'd forgotten it or at least had relegated to the darker chambers of her past) in fond, if excruciating detail—the wine, the fumbling, the broken, hapless way I'd looked at her when she'd left.

Closing my eyes now, I thought of the rain on the river, of my passport and medications, of my former student, the bright, if taciturn Nikhil. I checked the time. Tomorrow I'd be in England again. I pictured the busy High Street there, the view of rooftops and spires from the top of Carfax Tower.

It was true, I'd loved my time in Oxford—the bookstores, the pubs, the lazy evening walks along the river.

And I'd loved my time with Celeste.

*Celeste.*

We'd met, one hot summer morning, on the train ride to London, where I was going to meet a friend. I remembered the dress she was wearing, an airy celadon green, and I remembered her scent—a subtle, if beguiling medley of sunscreen, perfume, and sweat. Surreptitiously, I'd watched her as she'd arranged her things around her (her bag, her phone, and a book called *Archipelago* by a poet named Antonella Anedda), then slipped off her shoes, a pair of dark leather sandals, so that, like a child, a girl, she could tuck her legs beneath her.

"My name's Celeste," she'd said at once, extending a slender hand for me to shake. I remembered the flash in her eyes. "My mother named me after the Cuban singer, Celeste Mendoza. Though God knows why, for I can neither sing nor dance!"

"Who's Celeste Mendoza?" I'd inquired, intrigued.

"Celeste Mendoza? Why, the Queen of Guaguancos!" she'd cried. "Here, have a look at this," she'd insisted, pulling out her phone on which she'd played for me a short black and white video of the singer performing at the Nacional Hotel in Havana in 1963. She'd leaned so close to me I'd felt her breath upon my neck. When it was over she'd looked at me and grinned. "You see the resemblance? I tell you, my mother was mad!"

I was wide awake now. I could feel the adrenaline coursing through my veins, and went to the kitchen, poured myself a scotch, then switched on the television. I flipped quickly through a number of news programs, the highlights of a baseball game, and a crime show set in Oslo, when I caught the tail-end of a film called *Marriage Italian Style* with Marcello Mastroianni and Sophia Loren. It was a film I'd seen before, with someone somewhere, though I couldn't remember much about it, the characters, the plot, and watched it now, at least what remained of it, with a tender, if vacant delight.

I myself had never really thought about marriage. Or rather I'd thought about it, one has no choice but to think about it, but had never given it much notice, much shrift. My parents had gotten divorced when I was six, my father having never remarried, so that marriage, as a convention, had always seemed strange to me, an accord, an arrangement, the rewards of which were often hard for me to discern. True, quite a number of my friends and colleagues were married, some of them happily, it seemed, and some of them less so, though I might never have explained it.

It was Mary's relationship with Richard that was the truest gauge of the matter for me, and from which I couldn't help deducing a number of stark and troubling facts. Since they'd met, I'd spent years in their company,

*51*

strange, joyous, often starkly intimate times. I'd argued with them, eaten meals with them, celebrated holidays with them, and, before the boys were born, had enjoyed many a reckless summer with them in their house on Long Beach Island. I'd seen and heard it all.

As couples went, I felt I knew them as well as I knew anyone alive. Over the years, by a process largely unwitting, unconscious, I'd become a cipher for them, an amanuensis of their thoughts and behaviors, so that little or nothing escaped me now—not a sigh, a twitch, not a sniffle or snort, not so much as a flicker in their usually flickerless eyes. I saw it all, I marked it all, which is not to say that I understood it, that I understood *them*. I didn't, I don't.

Certainly I knew Mary best. We'd been friends for so long we'd often had trouble distinguishing ourselves, so that at times I'd found that to be angry at her was to be angry at myself.

I knew less about Richard. For all his gregariousness, for all his warmth and equanimity, there was something chary, even circumspect, about him. While I'd never been able to square Mary's sense of him with the man I knew and loved, she was not wrong about the reserve one sometimes felt in him, an impression, which—even as he confided in one, even as he squeezed one's shoulder, one's hand—made one feel as if one were standing at the edge of a dark and placid sea.

Educated in New York, Richard had been a brilliant, charismatic student. At the age of twelve, he'd decided to learn Chinese, had found himself a tutor, and had achieved what was at least an academic proficiency in the language by the time he was seventeen, soon after which he'd packed his bags and moved to Taiwan, to the cramped apartment of a professor in Taipei with whom (much to his parent's dismay) he'd been corresponding for years. He meditated, loved cats, slept naked, and enjoyed little more on a rainy Sunday morning than to listen to opera—to arias of Gigli, Tebaldi, and Callas.

Such and more did I know about him, a rattlebag of facts that altogether seemed misleading, somehow, like decoys or distractions, like so many red herrings he'd left for the finding on his trail. He had a way of telling you everything without telling you anything, that is, anything substantial, *revealing*. Yet somehow one was satisfied. It was like a sleight of hand with him: one knew it was a ruse, a trick, and still one marveled at it.

Only Mary's unhappiness, the sometimes violence of her misery, had given me pause. Indeed, I'd often thought of broaching the subject with him, of asking him directly about her, as a means of better understanding him and their relationship, but had never said a word. As much as I loved them, their marriage was *theirs*; it was none of my business.

I thought again of the quotation by Malraux. It seemed poignant enough when thinking of Richard, but what about Mary herself? And what about me? Aside from my love of her, what had I to hide—and from whom?

The movie had ended and I switched off the television. Briefly I thought of texting Mary and telling her something to reassure her, but was in no mood for a lengthy back-and-forth and switched off my phone. I'd text her in the morning, I decided, perhaps just as I was boarding the plane.

My first impression Oxford was that I'd never been there before. So odd, so *ulterior*, did it seem to me that for a moment I had to stand there at the end of the crowded railway platform until I gathered my wits. I was like a character in a film who arrives at a familiar station after a long time away, as after a war in which he'd been wounded, or as following a lengthy sojourn in the name of some calling, some god, only to discover that there was no one there to meet him, no mother or father, no wife or lover, no brother or daughter or son, that in fact he was not expected at that hour on that day, or indeed at any hour on any day, but had simply imagined it all (the embraces, the laughter), perhaps had dreamed it the night before, a vision, a conceit, that had somehow survived the violence of his waking, so that he was still bewitched by it when the train pulled out of the station and he found himself alone. As such a man, I resisted the urge to look around me now, to betray my confusion, and followed the last of the commuters as they made their way out.

The day was warm, unseasonably so. But for some high, ribbon-like clouds the sky was clear. According to my phone, it was just a ten-minute walk to my hotel and I set out for it at a brisk pace, pulling my suitcase behind me, though it wasn't long before I realized my mistake. Hungry, harried by the trip, I found myself overwhelmed by the heat, and by the traffic and noise. I was struck by the sheer number of people, tourists mostly, pressing their way through the starkly foreign streets. Certain images flashed through my mind (a footpath, an archway, a thicket of yellow roses) as though they were struggling to compose themselves into something I might remember, might know, some impression or experience that would cinch the net on the past for me, anneal the atoms in the crystal lattice of my brain, but they scattered at once, the images, so that I had to take refuge in the doorway of an empty Thai restaurant to catch my breath.

I felt silly, given the distance, but hailed a taxi anyway, and in minutes I was standing before the door of my hotel.

Mary had chosen well for me. Near the roar and bustle of the Covered Market was the short, tranquil lane of St. Michael's. The only commerce at that end of the street, besides the hotel itself, was a coffee shop, a small Mexican restaurant, and the Three Goats Heads pub, out front of which a half a dozen people were eating their lunch.

The woman at the hotel desk greeted me warmly, if without feeling. Her name—so I read on her tag—was Ms. Bent.

Mary had booked for me a small double room on the third and highest floor of the building, into which I was shuffled by one of the assistants there, a slender, dark-skinned youth with an accent I couldn't place. At the door, I offered him a tip, which he politely refused, only to return for it a moment later, grinning sheepishly and nodding his head.

Alone in the room, I unpacked my clothes, what few of them I'd brought with me, before arranging my books and laptop on the little desk by the window.

Across the street I could see a compound of sorts, all but concealed behind a high stone wall. I discovered on the internet that it was the grounds of the famous Oxford Union, one of Britain's oldest debating societies, best known, at least recently, for hosting such controversial speakers as the neo-Nazi, John Tyndall, and the Holocaust denier, David Irving.

My room, called 'The Trellis Room', had been furnished in a soothing, English style, with brown walls, brown drapes, and a patterned brown throw at the foot of the bed.

There was a fireplace, too, with a darkly stained mantel, a reading chair, and a chest of drawers with clear glass pulls.

The bathroom, by contrast, was distinctly modern. With its sleek-looking toilet and sink, its glassed-in shower, and its freestanding white tub, I could have been in any large city in the world.

Hungry as I was, I brushed my teeth, then took a hot, leisurely shower. I listened to the local news on the television as I dressed (a brief segment on the weather, a report on a new parking regulation, then a story about a competition to name the mascot outside a local butcher shop), so that by the time I left the hotel I was feeling every bit myself again.

I decided to try the pub down the street. Yet rather than sit at one of the little tables out front, most of which were in direct sunlight, I descended into the pub itself, a cool dark room of wood and gilding and brass. The walls, what little I could see of them in the moment, were covered with old photographs and prints. I placed my order at the bar, where the woman drew me a pint of the local bitter, a beer I hadn't tasted in years.

I'd not yet texted Mary, I knew she'd be anxious, and took the time now to do so. Only after I'd finished my message to her did I notice the sign by my table prohibiting the use of electronic devices inside the pub and promptly switched off my phone.

For more than an hour I sat there in the somber coolness of the pub, pleased simply to watch the customers come and go, and to listen to the waiters, students likely, as they talked about some recent local match.

It was strange to be back in Oxford. I thought I'd never return, and tried now to recall my time here, that brilliant, painful summer, bidding the memories and feelings to come.

As a fellow at nearby St. John's College, I'd been provided with a single room and bathroom overlooking the crooked Lamb and Flag Passage that linked St. Giles' to Blackhall Road. At the time, I'd been working on a book about a Resistance network of scientists and lawyers in Paris known as 'Le Musée de L'Homme', which had been infiltrated and destroyed by a Vichy supporter in 1942. As part of the fellowship, I'd been granted access to both the college's Old Library, with its timbered ceilings and pew-like seats, and the more Victorian-style Laudian Library, or Inner Library, where the books and papers of A.E. Housman were kept. It was in the latter that I'd spent the bulk of my time while here, reading and thinking and making notes.

Every day had been more or less the same: I'd

showered, eaten breakfast, read for three or four hours, then made my way to the pub at the corner, The King's Arms, for lunch and a pint of ale before popping into Blackwell's to browse the well-stocked shelves. Only then did I return to the college, to its peaceful gardens, for a nap beneath a towering copper beech.

I finished my beer now and paid the bill. The fish and chips had renewed my energy, restored my mood, so that I was eager to reacquaint myself with the city. I wanted to see the Bodleian Library—it would be my north star—and set out for it at once, wending my way through the crowds on Broad Street until I reached the Sheldonian Theatre, through the familiar grounds of which I pressed my way until I was standing in the ancient Old Schools Quad. It was much as I remembered it—the Tower of Five Orders, the modern heads, the pale and time-worn stone.

Mary and I had often talked about libraries. Ever since she was young she'd sought them out, had found in them a shelter from the world, a solace for presentiments and feelings for which, at least at the time, she hadn't the power, the autonomy, to account. She loved the newly renovated library at the women's college where she taught and could often be found there, in one of the carrels, where she liked to do her work.

It was from her that I'd first learned about the French

philosopher, Bachelard, who in his study, *The Poetics of Space*, had extolled such havens, now few and far between, those safeholds, those sanctums, that allowed for daydreaming, that protected the dreamer in her dreams, in 'the being of within'. He'd argued that the values that belong to daydreaming were essential to the health of humanity, to our sense of connection with the greater anthropocosmic world.

It was on one such occasion, when we were sitting in her office overlooking Claremont Avenue, with its old wooden cabinets, wide-silled windows, and patched wooden floor, that she'd told me the author, Goytisolo, a man who'd also loved libraries, if differently, *perversely*, reading aloud to me, by way of example, the trenchant, uproarious part in his novel, *Reivindicación del Conde Julián*, in which the scornful narrator recounts for the reader, from his seaside eyrie in Tangier, his former habit of collecting dead insects (spiders, bees, ants, cockroaches, and clumsy, thick-bodied flies) in a little drawstring pouch which, once full, he'd snuck with him into the great libraries of Spain in order to crush the bugs (singly, doubly, sometimes a half a dozen at a time) between the pages of their oldest, most hallowed books—those dusty tomes of rhetoric and purity he so thoroughly abhorred. Tears in her eyes, she'd shared with me the narrator's secret treachery in page after page of his barbarous, anarchical prose: "...reaching for the first volume in the pile and depositing an ant and six flies inside it: in the middle of the crucial scene between Cassandra and the Duke: I could not love thee, dear, so much loved I not honor more: suddenly closing the volume and crushing these seven insects: very cautiously, however, so the custodian doesn't catch you in the act: then opening the book and unhurriedly contemplating the result, with the finical appetite of the connoisseur: squashed flat, their guts splattered all over: indelible stains blotting the dramatic episode, contaminating it with their sluggish viscous flow..." I remembered Mary's profile that evening, as book in hand and giddy with pleasure she'd read on to me: "...and now you choose the paper-bound anthology of the thousand best poems in the language: the 'Dos de Mayo', the resoundingly patriotic sonnet of Enrique López Alarcón!: you can barely keep from drooling as you place the massive corpse of a horsefly on top of it, and zap!: *consummatum est*: the perfect hendecasyllable is shattered, the grandiloquent tercet blotted out: you stifle a triumphant cry..."

As it wasn't possible for me to enter the Bodleian without a reader card or as a member of an official tour, I returned to Broad Street, then crossed directly to Blackwell's bookshop, which I was pleased to see was doing a brisk business at that hour.

As always, I considered the books on display in the large bay windows. Celeste and I had spent many hours browsing the shelves there, often not leaving the shop until closing time, when we'd made our way back to my room at St. John's.

It had been on just such a night that she'd died of a cerebral hemorrhage, of a bleeding in her brain. The memory was acutely, disturbingly plain. We'd eaten at a popular restaurant in town where the wine had tasted sour to her, the risotto chalky, like paste. I remembered she'd felt a tingling in her fingers and lips. She'd not mentioned them again, the sensations, but had seemed very much herself again by the time we'd left the restaurant, laughing and teasing me and generally enjoying the soft summer air.

I sniffed the air now. For all the traffic, it smelled greenly of rivers and trees. For some reason it reminded me of Richard—Richard! Good God, I'd forgotten all about him!

Panicked, I scanned the faces around me, then ducked inside the shop.

The place was crowded and I pressed my way to the back, then down the stairs to the basement, where I stood heaving beside the handsome, red-bound works of Pliny. What had I been thinking, just standing there, gaping at the window like a tourist? What if Richard had seen me, tapped me on the shoulder? What would I have said?

Pulling a book at random from the shelves, a copy of Pindar's *Nemean Odes*, I surveyed the customers at hand, none of whom seemed to have noticed me. I could hardly believe it: only hours in the city and already I'd let down my guard! I'd have to be more careful.

I tried to picture Richard at the moment, reading or eating, perhaps browsing in a shop nearby. Mary had given me a number of possible addresses for him—of a house in Jericho, where he often stayed; of an office at Balliol College, just next door, in which sometimes he worked; and of the China Centre on Canterbury Road, in the archives of which he frequently conducted his research. She'd told me that the Centre had a tearoom he liked and had urged me to look for him there.

Yet I was in no mood to look for him, not yet. I didn't want to think of him at all. Instead I peered outside, then, as if by habit, by reflex, hurried my way up St Giles', past the Martyrs' Memorial, until I was standing in the shade of sycamores before the ancient gate of St. John's. The old porter was gone, his lodge replaced by a shielded security desk, complete with computers, CCTV monitors, and a pair of surly-looking guards.

The guards, as it turned out, were quite friendly,

welcoming me back to the college and granting me permission to reacquaint myself with the gardens there.

After the bustle of the streets, I was pleased to wander the empty grounds, with their air of ancient seclusion, to admire the flowers and shrubs, and to find the beech tree at the foot of which I'd taken my daily naps. It was all as I'd remembered it.

From somewhere nearby came the tolling of bells.

Seated comfortably on a bench at the back of the garden, by a rustic section of wall, I pulled out my copy of *Primera memoria*, thinking I might sit there until I finished it, but was too excited to make sense of the story, the words.

Instead I mused about my time there, in Oxford, what now seemed like a lifetime ago, about the walks I'd taken, about the many languid hours I'd spent thinking and dreaming on a bench in that same garden, a book or journal in hand. I'd read hundreds of pages that summer in my effort to understand the life and destruction of the short-lived resistance movement, 'Le Musée de L'Homme', a name adopted from the museum itself.

At the heart of my study was the ethnologist, museum director, and group founder, Paul Rivet. With his bald pate and owl-eyed glasses he was an unlikely hero.

By training a physician and scholar, he'd spent years, in

fact the better part of his career, following his return from South America, contesting the increasingly racist anthropology of the times, especially as it he'd found embraced by many of his colleagues, fellow philologists and ethnologists in Austria and Germany and France.

Even under the Occupation, Rivet had spoken widely about the dangers of scientific racism, insisting, in both his writings and his museum lectures, that human beings—for all their apparent differences—were a single, indivisible whole. Yet he was hardly so naive as to think that the Nazis and their collaborators would heed his claims. Working late at night with a cadre of scientists and lawyers, he'd set up a makeshift headquarters for the movement in the museum's basement, then cluttered with mummies, pots, weapons, and skulls, where they'd trained new dissidents, organized escape routes for Jews and other prisoners, gathered military intelligence for the Allied Forces, translated speeches by Churchill and Roosevelt, and printed for distribution an eclectic assortment of posters, leaflets, pamphlets, and flyers, as well as weekly editions—mostly broadsheets—of an early antifascist newspaper called *Résistance*.

Then one day, not long after the group was founded, Rivet learned by way of the radio that the Vichy government, under Marshal Pétain, had stripped him of his museum post. Clearly the group had been exposed;

someone—the faces had flitted through his mind—had betrayed them. Yet veteran that he was, he'd wasted no time trying to identify the culprit, but had packed his bags and fled to Colombia that same night, the Gestapo hard on his heels. Once settled in Bogotá, he'd headed up the local committee of General de Gaulle's government-in-exile, providing intelligence and logistical support to his comrades in the Resistance back home.

By the spring of that same year, the Gestapo had not only ransacked the museum—Rivet's life's work—but, with the help of German intelligence, the *Abwehr*, had rounded up nearly every one of his fellow *résistants*, most of whom had been tortured, then killed.

The book, once published, had been moderately well-received, at least for a work of its kind. For weeks, I'd followed the reviews in the journals I knew, the book had seemed to be gaining some traction, when all at once it had vanished from sight.

I pictured it as it had stood on the shelf in Mary's mother's kitchen, there beside *The Joy of Cooking*, my study of the Klaus Barbie trial, *The Way to Cook*, *Microwave Gourmet*, my book on the French double agent, Mathilde Carré, and, with its iconic lobster on the cover, an autographed copy of *La Technique*.

Eyes closed now I gritted my teeth. I was forty-three

years old; I was single and lonely and tired. And here I was, in England, sent to spy on one of my oldest and dearest friends. What the hell had happened? Where had I gone wrong?

To the best of my knowledge, I'd done what everyone else had done. I'd passed through most, if not all, of the commonplace phases. What signs, what cues, had I missed?

I looked about me now. The light had changed; on the path, not far from where I sat, two elderly women in Easter-looking hats were admiring a thick skirting of white hydrangeas. They didn't appear to have noticed me, their voices crisp with their pleasure, their joy. I watched them for a spell until, arm-in-arm, still talking, they wandered away.

It was nearly three o'clock by the time I left St. John's. The instant I switched on my phone I saw that I had three new messages—all of them from Mary. She was happy to know I'd arrived safely and that I liked the hotel. Again she thanked me for being here. Please be careful, she said.

The beer had made me groggy and for a moment I stood outside the college gate, bewildered again by the traffic and noise, by the seemingly endless stream of tour buses roaring their way toward the center of town.

I had nowhere to go, nowhere to be. I hadn't a plan of

any kind, a fact that surprised me now. For all my antici-
pation of the trip, I'd scarcely given a thought to what I'd
do once I was actually here. How should I begin? What
was my strategy to be?

I'd never spied on anyone before, at least as an adult.
Should I disguise myself, wear a trench coat and sunglasses? Perhaps a wig and a thick black mustache? It all
was too ridiculous to think about, and again I considered
calling off the whole thing. It would be easy now, I reasoned plainly, now that I was here in Oxford. All I'd have
to do was to text Mary and tell her that I'd changed my
mind, that I was returning home, that our friendship was
over and done.

Bitterly, I thought of my years of patient devotion to
her, and to her boys, of the untold hours I'd spent con-
soling her, praising her, and listening to her talk. And for
what?

She hardly knew me at all. She thought she did; she
thought she knew me well, and often said as much to
others, to colleagues who inquired about my work, to her
mother and her brother, and even to her boys, in whose
presence she liked to tease me with the things she knew.

The truth was, we'd never really been friends. Over
the years, she'd rarely ever asked me about myself, about
my work, my love life, my health. She thought little about

the things that mattered most to me; she simply didn't care. Even her praise of me, infrequent as it was, had usually proven selfish in the end. I'd tell her that and more when I texted her, that I was finished with trying to please her, done with playing her lackey, her fool. *You've humiliated me for the last time*, I swore aloud to myself, as I made my way back toward the center of town, and was so caught up in the fury of it all that I nearly collided with a man on a bike.

The altercation was jarring, the young man abusive, irate, so that by the time I collected myself and started off again my righteousness and anger had passed. Of course I would always be her fool. I knew it as well as I knew my own birthday, my name. If Mary was to blame for my being here, I was even more so. After all, she hadn't forced me to come; I'd agreed to do the job for her. I'd practically leaped at the chance!

And what about Richard? Surely he was also to blame—but how, and for what? I didn't know.

Now I tried to recall him—his smile, his composure, his voice. He was one of the kindest, most beneficent men I'd ever known. Everywhere he went he cast a spell, drawing people into his wake with an ease, a nearly holy complaisance, that bewildered even his most ardent rivals and foes. It was the quality Mary hated most about him.

"Only a man could be that poised," she'd quipped to

me one evening when he'd gotten out of the rental car to open the trunk. We'd just returned from a day at the beach and were feeling hot and irritable. A child had nearly drowned that afternoon, his mother hysterical, pulling at her hair and clawing at her skin, when there amidst the waves we'd seen Richard's head, his unmistakable head, and in his arms the boy, pale and gasping like a newborn, a fish.

Richard incensed her. Some days—she was not proud of it—she prayed he would stumble, lose his way, that he'd trip and stagger and fall. She longed for him to overstep himself, to be censured, admonished, reproached. Once and for all, she wanted to see him shaken, to see him weep, to rant and rave, to doubt his own judgments, his mind. She liked to picture him in handcuffs, head bowed before a judge, for then she could pity him, then she could hope to raise him up.

Yet such wishing was in vain. No matter how often she confronted him, with what slanders, what threats, she could never get a rise out of him. When she shouted, when she paced the room before him, fretting and fuming and biting her nails, he never responded in kind, only listened gravely, nodding his head until she stopped, until she ran down like the mechanism in some garish wind-up toy. Such efforts were pointless, she knew. Even as she cursed him, as her eyes bulged, as the blood ran riot in her temples and ears, she knew he would not react to her, to her provocations, not then, not ever—except perhaps to hold her, kiss her, and stroke her florid cheeks.

"It's funny, I don't know that I even love him anymore," she'd confessed to me one night, not long after we'd returned from France. It was the first time she'd mentioned him in weeks. "I mean, what the hell is love anyway? Longing? Devotion? Forbearance?" She'd scoffed at the notions. "Of course, that's what we tell ourselves, we must, but the truth is something else, what we call love just a pact we make, a deal with the Devil, a hedge against the pain and sorrow that is certain to come. We'll do anything, *believe* anything, as long as there's someone to cook for, to talk to, to hold us each night in our beds. *Love*—it's nothing but a posture, a pose, the frilly flipside of our own most-certain dread." I'd thought she'd finished, when wearily, drawing out the words, she'd said, "Yet it gets its hooks in you, you know..."

Now I checked the time on my watch. At that hour Mary would be in her kitchen, drinking coffee and flipping through *The New York Times*. It wasn't too late to call the whole thing off, I argued frankly, as I made my way back toward the Bodleian; I'd end it all right now, before I got even more entangled, before I got trapped. Once back at the hotel, I'd simply tell her I'd made a mistake in agreeing to undertake the trip for her, that, as soon as I could manage it, I'd be flying back home.

What had I been thinking? It wasn't I who needed her; I'd been alone for years. It was she who needed *me*. The realization was sobering, I felt better for it, and had gotten as far as the next block, having resolved to dispatch the matter as soon as I reached my hotel, when there by the bus stop was Richard!

There was no mistaking him, his tall, lithesome build, his clear-framed glasses, and his thick gray mane of hair. Dressed differently than usual, in light-colored slacks and a striped t-shirt, he was chatting easily with a young, dark-haired woman in sunglasses, a woman perhaps half his age, occasionally touching her arm as if to reassure her, as if to affirm something he'd told her, some promise, some secret, some gift. Who knew?

What was clear, what was certain in their every gesture, was that they knew each other well, an intimacy that was nothing if not sexual.

Was it to be this easy? I marveled. It seemed too good, too pat, to be true.

Quickly I snapped a few photographs of them with my phone and was crossing the street to get a better angle on them when their bus arrived, blocking my view.

Impatiently, I pressed my way through the blindly milling crowd, hoping to get a better look at the woman, at what she was wearing, and at the expression on Richard's face, but by the time I reached the bus stop they were gone.

Only then did it occur to me that I should have noted the number of the bus they'd taken. It might have proven useful to me. Based on the map at the bus stop, a snarl of brightly colored lines, it could have been the city6 to Wolvercote via Jericho, the city9 to Risington, or the city46 to Great Milton. There was no way to tell, and I cursed myself in my frustration. What if I never saw him again? It was possible. What would I tell Mary?

I'd have to come up with a plan. Certainly I couldn't rely on fate, on the chance of our being in the same place at the same time again. I couldn't risk it, the prospect of being seen by him, but would have to be more thoughtful, more deliberate in my approach.

I had the addresses Mary had given me; I'd scout them out tomorrow. Yes, that was it: once back at the hotel, I'd devise a schedule of sorts, posting myself outside each of the locations for a certain number of hours each day, until I spotted him again, it was bound to happen, when I'd follow him at a distance, making a note of his circuits, his routine. Once I knew his habits, where he went and *when*, it would be but a couple of days before I could return to New York.

Seated at the desk back in my hotel room, I examined the photographs I'd taken of them at the bus stop, hoping to discover more about the young woman in sunglasses, and about the specific nature of their relationship. I didn't doubt they were lovers; I knew they were; I'd seen the signs before. I simply wished to err on the side of caution. After all, it was possible I'd been mistaken, that my eyes had deceived me. Given my predisposition to find him guilty, that is, my very presence here in Oxford, it was not unreasonable to think that, like a scholar who, through a series of minor academic delinquencies, discovers exactly what he'd set out to find, I might have misjudged their behavior, might have seen only what I *wanted* to see, what Mary had *prepared* me to see, to the exclusion of everything else.

Then of course there was the matter of my own uncertain motives here. Surely, I wanted to help Mary, to confirm or repudiate her suspicions, and, in that way, to finally put her mind at ease. Still, I couldn't deny the pleasure I'd felt the night she'd tendered her request to me, the sense that, after years of patient waiting, my time had come at last.

I looked again at the photographs. Yes, it was possible I'd misread their behavior. Perhaps they were only colleagues or friends, I considered patiently, judiciously, when briefly, as an exercise, I imagined them at a restaurant together, eating pasta, sipping wine, saw them talking smartly about literature and politics, pictured them naked and groaning in bed. I couldn't help it; their behavior at the bus stop had been so starkly carnal I couldn't even pretend to be wrong.

In one of the photographs I'd captured the young woman in a smiling, three-quarter view. She was pretty, familiar even, with dark hair and slender, lightly painted lips. Surely it was not unusual for someone her age to be attracted to an older man, especially one as handsome and cultured as Richard. Loathe as I was to admit it, they seemed an easy, natural fit.

For a time, not knowing what else to do, I remained seated at the small painted desk by the window, checking my email, shopping for shoes and shirts, and reviewing my editor's suggestions about the opening chapter of my book about the SS massacre at Oradour-sur-Glane.

I'd been struggling for days with a particularly difficult part of it, a section in which, through the use of the pioneering work of French philosopher and sociologist, Maurice Halbwachs, I was attempting to argue the importance to collective memory of what he'd called 'spatial frameworks', that is, to describe the necessary link between extraordinary events and the specific places in which they occurred. Perhaps nowhere, short of Auschwitz and Hiroshima, was there a clearer case-in-point than Oradour-sur-Glane. Indeed, its remains, the more than forty acres of charred and crumbling buildings, had become a pilgrimage site since the war, complete with miracles and relics, a secular shrine in a cult of anger, longing, and pain.

*Recueillez-vous.*

Upon my editor's suggestion, I'd recently added a short description of the site itself, as one might approach it on foot, and briefly reviewed what I'd written:

> The visitor to Oradour usually enters the ruins at one or two iron gates situated at either end of the old main street. Approaching on the road from Limoges, one can park in a small lot at the lower entrance, cross the bridge over the Glane, and walk in below the church. However, most cars and tour buses continue along the highway. The view opens out. To the right is a broad view of the ruins, while straight ahead the tower of the new church perches on the crest of a small hill. As the main road curves sharply west, bypassing the new town, one turns off into an unpaved lot between the new town and the ruins, only a few steps from the upper entrance. Just inside the gate, a young woman employed by the Historic

Monuments Service sells postcards, slides,
and books.

I liked what I had so far and took the time now to consider the many photographs I'd brought along with me in
a large accordion folder. Most of them were purely func-
tional images, hasty, thumbnail shots of the buildings
themselves—of the garage, the post office, the barns, the
marketplace, the girls' school, the boys' school, and the
church, with its blackened transepts and nave, though
there were photographs of people, too, of those still living
and those now mutely, helplessly dead.

Yet the photographs that most intrigued me were the
ones I'd taken of the various artifacts to be found within
the little museum there, a drab, low-lying building that one
entered through a heavy stone portal. In the center of the
hushed and hallowed space, four glass cases, their shelves lit
dully from within, had been arranged in a circle for better
viewing. Within them one discovered, as in the memorial
museum in Hiroshima, a random, banal, sometimes striking
assortment of everyday objects, of *things*: pocket watches,
jackknives, identity papers, rings, toys, coins, buttons, thim-
bles, keys, spoons, nails, ration cards for wine and tobacco,
stamps, letters, postcards, locks of hair, and a crudely lami-
nated snapshot of the local soccer team from 1944.

For a time I studied the various photographs and

made some notes, when, feeling restless, I replaced them in the folder.

I was hungry and considered the light outside, the sky a dark, crepuscular blue. Slipping my book and laptop into my bag, I made my way back down the stairs, nodding politely to Ms. Bent who, suddenly interrupted, flashed me a brusque, admonitory look.

I was thinking of getting a curry somewhere, or perhaps a kebab, when I felt a stronger, more bewildering pull.

It had never occurred to me to return there. What good, what purpose, could it serve? After all, it was only a restaurant, a space like any other, with waiters and tables and chairs. What was there to be gained by seeing it again? It was foolish, I knew.

The restaurant, if I remembered correctly, was only minutes away. At the other end of St. Michael's I turned right then left at once on George Street, still busy at that hour, when there I saw it, with its blue facade and red awnings, at the end of Bulwarks Lane.

Celeste had been the one who'd chosen the restaurant that night, who'd stood patiently by the entrance as I'd examined the menu in the window. And it was she who'd chosen our table, a table for two beside a curtain of dangling lights. She'd gotten word that morning that a collection of her poems had been accepted for publication by a small, independent press in London. The dinner was to be our celebration of the news, and tacitly, at least for me, of our future together, our life.

Now the restaurant was practically empty. But for an elderly couple at a table in one corner and a young woman with braids who appeared to be waiting for someone, there were no other customers but me.

Before the waiter could seat me, I chose the table at which Celeste and I had eaten, years before, the one beside the curtain of dangling lights. Yet rather than take the chair in which I'd sat that evening, the one facing out toward the street, I settled myself in the one facing inward toward the open-plan kitchen and bar. The effect was instantly disconcerting, so much so that when the waiter handed me a menu and asked me what I'd like to drink, I could only stammer and blink.

Fortunately, he was not fazed; filling my water glass, he assured me I needn't hurry. I was free to take my time.

I sipped the cool water and took a long, deep breath, when suddenly, amidst the sounds of cooking and the clatter of plateware, I became aware of the music being pumped into the room around me through invisible speakers, something airy, springlike, baroque. I couldn't remember having heard any music the night I'd dined here with Celeste, though they must have been playing something. Restaurants always played *something*.

I remembered Celeste had brought with her a book that evening, one she'd been reading all day, and had set it on the table beside her, as she might have her cellphone or purse. She'd been talking about it for days, the story, it had been much on her mind, some wry, intelligent novel by Murdoch, Brookner, or Drabble. I remembered it clearly—its cover, its condition, a thick well-thumbed paperback called *The Eye of the Needle*, or something Biblical like that, though the story itself was not religious, not by far. Celeste would not have stood for it, such characters, such inklings, for she'd deplored the faithful, particularly in fiction—their bowing and scraping, the wretched, doleful look in their eyes. She'd felt that life itself was humbling enough.

In the novel there was a married man, a disaffected lawyer of some sort, who, through a series of commonplace events, finds his life entangled with that of a young mother and divorcée, a mad, long-suffering woman named Rose. There'd been something about the woman that had moved Celeste especially, something about her and her children in the ugly London suburb where they lived, which, the same thing, had moved the man himself, the lawyer in the novel, something raw, untoward about her that had shown a cold, bright light on his life.

I was trying to remember what it was about the woman, to recall the peculiar way that Celeste had described her to me, for I remembered it well, the force and tenor of her words, when I winced at the recollection of a certain image from the novel, from a passage she'd shared with me that night, the image of a man with hideous, battered wings huddled wretched and lonely on the branch of a tree. "And his spirit would hunch its feathered bony shoulders…"

Yes, I remembered that! It had gone something like that, I was sure. And there'd been something about a mesh, a net, in which he'd been captured, been caught.

Now I considered the menu before me. Celeste had ordered the seafood risotto with a caprese salad that night; yet oddly there was no listing for seafood risotto, nor for risotto of any kind. Perplexed, I signaled the waiter and asked him if they were serving risotto this evening, perhaps as a special, to which he'd replied that they were not. To the best of his knowledge, the restaurant had never served risotto.

I knew it wasn't true, but resisted the urge to correct him. He must be new to the place, I gathered calmly, taking another sip of water. After all, the turnover of waiters was high. Who knew, since my dinner here with Celeste, the management itself might have changed hands, and briefly I looked around for any sign of it, for adjustments in the lighting, the placement of the tables, the decor, for surely that would have explained it.

The reasoning was sound, yet suddenly I felt flushed; my pulse was racing, the room began to spin, and in my panic to breathe I rose abruptly from my chair, upsetting my glass of water.

I'd forgotten where the exit was, the direction from which I'd come, and lurched madly toward the kitchen, toward the startled face of one of the waiters, only to retrace my steps and scramble my way out the door.

Bewildered, aghast, I wandered blindly through the streets that night. I lost track of the direction, the hours, pushing my way through crowds of people, crossing a wide, wet meadow, when for a spell I followed an overgrown path along a mucky-smelling canal lined with empty, weathered boats.

By the time I reached the city center again, a square that seemed familiar to me, my feet were sore, my throat was parched, my stomach convulsed with hunger. Most of the shops were closed. It seemed there'd been a market that day, so that it was with a childish glee that I spied a kebab shop, Kebab King, its lights ablaze across the empty, cobbled square.

I WOKE TWICE THAT NIGHT, once to get a drink of water, for the kebabs had been quite salty, and once to check a text on my phone. It was a message from my friend Simone Sagnier in Limoges, letting me know she'd found an apartment for me in a newly renovated *mas* in the nearby town of Saint-Priest-sous-Aixe. She thought it would be the perfect place for me to work this summer, a retreat, *une idylle*, she'd called it, in which to finish my book. Briefly, she'd described the apartment's amenities, the wi-fi, the washer-dryer, the coffee machine, the tiny sunroom filled with shells and fossils and plants. She'd included some photographs as well.

The place looked fine to me—clean, airy, surely more spacious than I required. From there, she assured me, it was just a twenty-minute drive to Oradour-sur-Glane.

Over the course of my many visits to the Limousin, I'd grown fond of the region, especially of the old Roman city of Limoges, with its soaring cathedral and Art Deco railway station, le Gare des Bénédictins. It was there, by chance, that I'd met Simone. I'd wandered into the station one day, curious to see its interior and eager to escape the rain, when she'd handed me a flier. As an adjunct at the local university, she'd been part of an awareness campaign designed to pressure the university into adopting a clearer, stricter policy regarding sexual and gender-based harassment. Briefly lovers, we'd been friends ever since.

I'd never understood her affection for me, her gentle, unflagging patience with me and my ways. She was smart, accomplished: she taught photography, drank tequila, collected records, mostly jazz, and read novels in English, German, and Dutch. Skinny, flagrant as a boy, she was beautiful.

So what had happened between us? I didn't know; in recent years, I'd hardly given it a thought.

I thought about it now. Adjusting the showerhead, I thought about her—her wit, her breasts, her love of English roses. And I thought about the trips we'd taken together throughout the verdant countryside, the hills and woodlands and scenic river valleys, in her battered blue 'Le Car'.

Strangely, I couldn't remember us parting; I couldn't picture it. What had I said when I left?

I hadn't seen her in more than a year; somehow, the last

time I was there, in Limoges, our paths had never crossed. I'd been so busy, the trip itself so brief, that I'd never even thought of her—a fact that now struck me as strange.

Once showered I shaved and got dressed. My plan for the morning was to walk to the Chinese Centre in North Oxford; it seemed a lovely day for it.

Ms. Bent was not at the desk when I descended the stairs, and I slipped quickly out the door, pleased to have escaped her detection and eager to stretch my legs. Warm as it was, I walked briskly; the movement did me good.

For some reason, I'd chosen a shirt I'd never liked, a green one that chafed my neck, and thought briefly of returning to the hotel to change it but was impatient for a cup of coffee and something to eat.

As by instinct, I made my way north again on St. Giles, already busy at that hour, past the Martyr's Memorial, built to commemorate the burning of some bishops, the Ashmolean Museum, and finally the dark, familiar gate of St. John's, from where, with difficulty, I cut across a tangle of heavily trafficked streets to a bakery-cafe, I'd read about, on a narrow, cobbled lane just around the corner from Somerville College.

I ordered a black coffee and custard brioche, then settled myself at one of the small metal tables out front.

An elderly man in broken-back slippers was examining a newspaper he'd just pulled from a bin stuffed to overflowing with coffee cups and takeaway cartons, and I was thinking of getting a newspaper for myself at the shop across the way, when I remembered my behavior last night.

What in the world had come over me? I wondered. I'd never experienced such panic before, such a blinding loss of perspective, control, and suddenly felt vulnerable sitting there on the sidewalk in the early morning air. The birds chirped, the traffic roared at the end of the lane; it seemed that anything might happen.

Shaken, I checked my phone, gobbled the last of the brioche, then swallowed what remained of my coffee, though it burned my tongue. The instant I rose from the table it was claimed by three young women in hijabs, students surely, all talking on their phones.

From there the walk to the China Centre was brief.

Set back from the street in a handsome Victorian neighborhood of well-tended gardens and tall, yellow-brick houses, the Centre was surprisingly contemporary in design. I wasn't sure how to approach it, how close to get for fear of encountering Richard, so that for a time I hesitated by the bike rack at the end of the graveled drive.

Fortunately there was no one at the desk when I entered the building. Following a sign for 'The Wordsworth Tea Room', I found myself in a small exhibition hall, from the center of which rose a magnificent spiral staircase made of wood, glass, and steel. The room, on that overcast morning, was suffused with a watery English light.

From there, though a large double doorway, I could see, at the back of the building, a verdant curve of lawn scattered leisurely with tables and chairs. Directly to my right was the tea room itself, a spare, if elegant-looking cafe that was busy at the hour.

Discreetly I scanned the crowd inside, but there was no sign of Richard.

The question was where to position myself, so that I could see the people coming and going from the building without attracting their attention? Briefly I returned to the street to look for a perch near the gate, but in the largely residential neighborhood there was no obvious place where I could linger unseen. The best option, it seemed, was to position myself within the grounds themselves, to the right of the entrance, where there was a small planted area and parking lot for about half a dozen cars. Odds were he'd never look that way.

Settling myself on a low concrete wall behind a black

Mercedes, beside a thick green stand of bamboo, I took out the novel, *Primera memoria*, and read steadily, determined to finish it that day. I'd read for perhaps twenty minutes, not a soul had come or gone, when I heard voices, two men talking, and the crunch of their feet on the gravel. Sadly, neither of them was Richard and I returned to my book, pausing now and then to turn my face to the sun.

I was reading along, soothed by the mild sunshine and the buzzing of bees just behind me, when I came upon a passage, quoted verbatim from a book the narrator's cousin had discovered in their grandfather's room, a section describing the medieval Mallorcan practice of burning Jews in the village square: "What a sight it was to behold, the fire catching on their flesh, the flames licking through their innards, their bellies tearing open, flaring with demonic brilliance…"

I'd not expected it in a novel set on the island of Mallorca, even during the Spanish Civil War, so that the plates of history shifted slightly in my mind.

By noon, more than a dozen people had come and gone from the Centre. The Mercedes had been replaced by a minivan, a delivery vehicle of some sort, which itself had been replaced by a red BMW, the owner of which, a young Sikh with a fine black beard, had eyed me warily until he'd noticed my book.

For a while I'd texted back and forth with Mary, an erratic, largely desultory exchange, then with my brother, Michael, as well, whose second wife had just left him. He'd returned home from one day to find that she and all of her belongings were gone. What had seemed to bother him most was the fact that she hadn't left him a note.

"I mean, what the hell?" he'd despaired in one of a flurry of texts to me. "Married for six fucking years and she couldn't be bothered to leave me a note? A note, for God's sake! The least she owed me was a fucking measly note!"

By one o'clock I was seated with a newspaper and a pint of ale at one of the long wooden tables in The King's Arms, a pub I knew well. I was surprised to find the place nearly empty, given the hour, and spread out the paper before me.

At least forty-one people had been killed in an attack on a secondary school in Uganda, an attack believed to have been carried out by Islamic State militants; Brexit was to blame for rising inflation, claimed former Bank of England governor, Mark Carney; England's vital hedges were under threat due to budget cuts; and there was rampant flooding in the southern Chinese city of Yulin, following more than thirty-five hours of non-stop rain.

I'd never been to Yulin; the closest I'd gotten was

Guilin, to which I'd traveled with Richard, one summer, to see its famous limestone crags. For some reason the article had reminded me of Ellen Martin, a woman I'd met one day, at that same table, when I was here as a fellow at St. Johns. Seated by herself near the window, she'd welcomed me to join her, as all the other tables had been full. With her sensible, short-cropped hair, her scattered books and papers, and her collection of empty wine glasses, I'd assumed, in my benevolence, she was English.

As it turned out, she was from the States, a professor from Berkeley who, like me, was in Oxford on a fellowship, hers at Christ Church. She hadn't waited for me to get comfortable, to even a look at the menu, before she'd declared, "The wine here is awful. Trust me. I suppose you don't like flowers."

"Flowers?" I'd replied. "I like them well enough."

"Well enough for what?" she'd countered, appraising me sternly over the top of her glasses.

"Well enough for..." I'd sputtered, foolishly. "I mean, I like them very much."

That afternoon, once we'd made ourselves silly with wine, she'd taken me to see the flowers at the botanic garden, just across the street from Magdalen College. She'd known the garden well, having visited it almost every day since she'd arrived.

She'd taken me first to the conservatory, then to the Rain Forest House, then, finally, to the Euphorbia Garden with its more than 2,000 species, after which we'd sat for an espresso at the little concession there, from where she'd pointed out a pair of red kites, circling high above us in the sky.

She was writing a book, she'd told me, as we'd explored the old physic garden with its tidy, taxonomic beds, a study of spiritual mediums in the Kathmandu Valley of Nepal, where she'd lived for many years with her late husband, Ted. We'd just found a place on a bench at the back of the Lower Garden with its storybook view of Magdalen Tower, when she'd told me of her first visit to a Newar medium in a small house in Patan, now called Lalitpur.

"As I approached her doorway," she'd begun, wide-eyed, a look of wonder on her frank and ruddy face, "the first thing I noticed was the medium's mother-in-law, a scowling woman in her late fifties who was scrubbing a pile of laundry on the cement floor. Making my way up the stairs, I heard hymns of praise coming from a small room. I bent to enter and found myself facing a powerful woman dressed in red, seated on an enormous brass and wood throne. Curving snakes of brass coiled up the arms of the throne, and their heads formed a canopy for the head of the medium. Adorned with yellow jasmine and vermilion powder, a crown of leaves upon her head, the deity in the medium had been worshiped just as an image in a temple would be. She listened as people explained their troubles to her, received their offerings of food, money and flowers, and blessed them as they bowed to her feet." At that point Ellen had smiled. "To anyone used to seeing married Newar women in their usual roles as household drudges who are constantly bowing to those above them in the social hierarchy—which for some of the younger women can mean practically everybody—watching them get worshiped instead is quite startling!

"Of course, that's precisely what intrigues me," she'd explained at once, raising a finger to accentuate the point. "The lack of tradition behind it. You see, it's actually a recent phenomenon: most locals agree that mediums first appeared in the Valley roughly forty or so years ago, and now their numbers are increasing. Think about it: every year there are more and more!"

We'd enjoyed many such talks in the course of my our time together there in Oxford that summer, talks about flowers and birds, about fruit trees and grafting, and about the years she'd spent as a child in Kathmandu, where her father had served as the U.S. ambassador.

Once finished with the newspaper, I found myself hungry and ordered a ham and leek pie with onion gravy.

By then the place had gotten crowded with tourists, mostly boisterous young men in fancy sportswear and sunglasses, so that once I'd eaten I hastened my way back to Blackwell's across the street.

Remarkably, the shop seemed just as crowded as before, if not more so, so that I was forced to reach above and around people just to examine the books.

Fortunately, the selection was as good as ever. I found a paperback about Benares, the holy city of Hindus, by a man named Aatish Taseer; a thriller by Eric Ambler, set in the Balkans; a book called *The Undercurrents* by British-American art critic, Kristy Bell; and one for Mary, a guidebook of sorts, called *Lorca's Granada*, the introduction to which I couldn't help perusing in the coffee shop upstairs.

I didn't know much about Lorca, I'd read a few of his poems over the years, and found myself intrigued by his brief and tragic life. Particularly interesting to me was what he'd called "the aesthetic of the diminutive", that is, his pious attention to detail, to small and commonplace things.

I thought of Simone, of the gentle, carefree times we'd spent together in Limoges. There was a joy to her, a delight in the simple and obvious and plain, that made me wonder, once again, how we'd parted and why. Like my mother, she trusted people, or at least she didn't *distrust* them, didn't instantly ascribe a motive—a selfish motive—to every word and deed.

Yet her life, I knew, had not been easy. Her mother was French, from Grenoble—a nurse who'd spent three years in Oran, before returning to France, to Lyon, where she'd died of breast cancer at the age of forty-six.

It had been there, in Algeria, that she'd met Simone's father, a handsome, dark-eyed intern, whom, on the advice of a friend, she'd agreed to meet for dinner one night at a popular restaurant by the sea. They'd been together for less than a month, when he'd vanished altogether, never to be seen again. All Simone knew of him, apart from his eyes and the pale white scar on his lip, was that his name—'highly praised'—was Ahmed.

That was it! I realized in a flash. The young woman I'd seen with Richard yesterday had reminded me of Simone. It had bothered me all night, the connection, so much so that I'd still been thinking about it when I'd opened my eyes this morning.

Of course, they didn't actually look alike: consulting the photographs on my phone, it was clear that Simone was taller than the woman I'd seen with Richard, her hair thicker, her nose more pronounced, distinctive, more integral to her beauty and bearing. The appeal of the young woman I'd seen with Richard seemed to arise from something else, from some other aspect of her being, for she was certainly attractive—oddly, almost unsettling so. Still, there was *something* that bound them, I knew.

Finishing my coffee, I returned the cup and saucer to the counter, charged with a newfound sense of purpose. Tomorrow, first thing, I'd stake out the house in Jericho where Richard sometimes stayed when he was in Oxford. I had hunch I'd spot him there.

To pass the time until dinner, I took a stroll around Christ Church meadow, stopping now and then, to take in the view behind me and to sit by the river, at the far end of the meadow, on which, for a time, I watched a man and his wife on the deck of their narrow boat, working hard to remove the rust from the fittings with an assortment of copper wire brushes. They worked patiently, methodically, and without a word to each other, pausing now and then only to stretch their backs or to rinse off their hands.

I was watching them work, admiring the high white clouds in the sky, when I received a text from Mary, telling me that she was thinking of disappearing again, of taking the boys somewhere without telling Richard.

The last time she'd done it, the previous summer, he hadn't spoken to her for days, after which he'd made her promise not to do it again.

This time, she was thinking of taking them to Cape Cod, perhaps to Martha's Vineyard or Nantucket. She'd never been to the Cape and asked me what I knew of it, of the beaches, the food, of Provincetown, Wellfleet, and Truro.

Ever since she'd first convinced herself that Richard was deceiving her, she'd made an effort to deceive him in turn—petty, awkward, often self-defeating gestures which she'd usually come to regret. One day she might hide one of his books, toss the morning paper down the chute at the end of the hall, or snip a button from one of his favorite shirts, which later, despite herself, she'd offer to replace for him.

She'd gone so far, on one occasion, when he'd happened to leave his laptop open on his desk, to delete some of the text he'd been working on—a word here, a sentence there, an entire paragraph near the end.

She'd confessed these things to me one night last fall, after she'd had too much to drink. For my forty-third birthday, she'd taken me for cocktails and dinner at The River Cafe, from where we'd gazed in wonder at the Brooklyn Bridge that passed almost directly overhead, and out across the river at the densely clustered towers of lower Manhattan, briefly gilded by the light. We'd drunk Gibsons, eaten oysters and foie gras, then gorged ourselves on lobster, Nova Scotia lobster, served with squash and spinach and chard.

In recent months, Mary'd grown leery of me, of my relationship with Richard, of the nature of my allegiance to her, so that only rarely now, and usually under the influence of alcohol, did she ever really drop her guard with me. Whereas once she might have depended on my fidelity, on my blind, my *categorical* faith, at some point she'd detected a change in me, a shift in my tone, my demeanor, an irony, an ambivalence, that had forced her to restrain herself when we were together, to study me, to parse her words, to hesitate, equivocate, draw back. Even the way she looked at me now was different, so that at times I'd squirmed like a truant under her wry, distrustful gaze.

For she was not wrong about me; I *had* changed. Lately I'd grown impatient with her griping, her lamentations, so that some nights, when she'd called me on the phone, I'd barely listened to her, grading papers, scrolling through my email, and playing game after game of solitaire or chess. It wasn't that my feelings for her had changed; they hadn't, at least not fundamentally. It was something different, something else.

Briefly, the couple on the boat had disappeared inside, only to reappear with a hamper of cold cuts, bread, and pickles, with which they'd made themselves sandwiches, hers smaller, his larger, only to wash them down with glasses of chilled white wine.

Reluctant as I was to break the spell of the moment, I replied to Mary's text. I strongly discouraged her from going away with the boys, from doing anything rash. The boys, I knew, were in camp, the one they attended every summer at the zoo in Central Park, so that I pictured her alone in the apartment all day, fretting, smoking, and pacing the empty rooms. There was something caustic, even incendiary, about her grief that at times made me fear she would burst into flame.

Sitting there, I might have relished my distance from her, my ease alone by the Thames, I might have switched off my phone, had it not been for the young woman I'd seen with Richard yesterday. Unless in fact my eyes had deceived me, Mary was right about him. I had to admit it: she'd been right all along, so that once again I was forced to recalibrate my thinking. If I was no longer sure about her, as a person, could I ever be sure about him?

Briefly I thought of what I'd say to Mary when I returned, what words and phrases I'd use. I pictured her sobbing and scowling and nodding her head. And I thought of the boys, of what she'd tell them, of what they'd intuit on their own.

I was tired by the time I got back to my hotel. The text from Mary had soured my mood, so that I wanted nothing so much as to forget about her, about her and Richard, to lose myself in sleep. Yet the room at that hour was stifling, too hot for resting, even with the fan switched on high.

At a loss as to what to do, I took another shower, changed my clothes, then sat down at the little desk by the window to work, but within minutes I was perspiring again, unable to read or think. It was then that I remembered the pub across the street. I could see it from where I sat, and, quickly gathering some books in my bag, I hurried down the stairs.

I sat at the same table in the cool and gloomy basement. Even the waiter was the same.

After the first pint I felt better. I read a few pages in *Primera memoria*, glanced at the thriller by Eric Ambler, then settled on the book about Benares, there on the Ganges, a place, with its ghats and pilgrims, I'd long wished to see.

Like me, the author was from New York, or at least had lived there for a time. I thought his opening brilliant—the description of a dream he'd had one night that the city of Benares had been suprcimposed upon the geography of Manhattan, magically transforming his being, his view.

I read avidly for nearly an hour, raising my head only to get my bearings again or to order another pint.

I was moved by what I read, by the author's struggle—at

times so painful, so poignant—to make peace with his dark and troubled past. What was my Benares? I wondered. I thought of New York, I thought vaguely of Amsterdam, to which city my father's greater family had fled during the Inquisition, the Lurias, the Ezekiels, the de Castros. I knew the names, little more.

By the time I returned to my hotel, the room had cooled off nicely, and for a time I rested on the bed in a t-shirt and shorts, listening to music, watching videos, and checking the news. I thought again about Benares, and about Amsterdam, where I hadn't been in years, about the canals, the parks, about the gabled old houses with their waterlogged basements and steep-dark stairs.

A BREEZE WAS BLOWING, THE sky overcast, when I opened my eyes. The morning air smelled freshly of rain.

It was raining in fact by the time I left the hotel, so that, rather than camp out near the house in Jericho, where I was unlikely to find shelter, I made my way to the entrance of Balliol College on Broad Street, where I knew he liked to work.

By then the rain had picked up, it had only been sprinkling before, so that the only cover I could find was inside the ItaliAmo Cafe. From there, from my table near the window, I had a clear view of the entrance and the Porter's Lodge.

I ordered a cappuccino and a cornetto, which I enjoyed immensely, with the familiar pleasure I felt when on vacation, though the illusion didn't last. Once the rain let up, as it had almost immediately, the tiny shop was overrun with tourists, just disgorged from a nearby bus, who gobbled up the pastries and devoured scoop after scoop of gelato, though it was barely half past ten.

Irritated, distracted by the commotion, I finished my breakfast then slipped inside a small art supply shop next door, where I bought myself a journal and a couple of nice pens.

For a moment I stood there in the doorway, uncertain what to do. I couldn't remain there, I knew, I couldn't bear it, the people, the noise, and made my way north again toward St. John's, thinking I might sit for a while in the gardens there, if I the guards would let me, when I decided to continue on to the Parks instead, a large, lush commons along the Cherwell, where I was certain to find some peace.

Mary—it was one of the things I loved about her—had never been fazed by tourists, whether in New York, Madrid, or Paris, where the streets were often so thronged with foreigners, with people like us, that I was all but overwhelmed. What always felt to me like a siege of the city, a fury of eating, grabbing, buying, and photographing, amused her, delighted her, so that more than once in our weeks together in Paris, I'd nearly lost her in the crowds.

One of the first things she'd done upon our arrival there, before we'd even unpacked our bags, and despite my protest, my complaints about the timing, the weather, was to book us tickets on a *bateau mouche*, one of the large excursion boats designed for tourists that daily plied the Seine between the Rive Gauche and Rive Droite.

In fact it had been a rainy, miserable day, I'd had a toothache, we were hungry, our shoes and socks were wet—all of which had done nothing to discourage Mary, to dampen her mood. Cynical, impatient, as she could be, she'd been utterly charmed by our guide, an elderly man, a poet and grandfather named Enguerran, who'd occasionally broken into song in the midst of his descriptions of the sights (of Notre-Dame, Pont Neuf, the Tuileries, and the Musée d'Orsay), moody, mostly sentimental songs by Georges Brassens, Carlos Gardel, and Françoise Hardy. Mary has insisted that the boat ride was one of the best ways for her to get her bearings again, to renew her appreciation for a side of the city (the side that had so impressed her as a girl) she might otherwise fail to see.

She could be positively perverse about it. In the time we'd spent together there in Paris, she'd made a special effort to seek out those sights, listed in every online guide, to which tourists were most likely to flock, so that, in the midst of our pursuit of eccentric Goytisolo, of the hours we'd in archives and libraries, we'd toured Versailles, crowded our way into the Catacombs, eaten lunch at the McDonald's on the Champs-Élysées, and seen a show, a dreadful show, at the famous Moulin Rouge.

Yet there was no experience of the kind that Mary relished more than that of crowding into the large, naked room at the Louvre to look at the Mona Lisa. What she loved, for she'd seen the painting before, was simply to listen to the comments of the people around her, no matter the language, for the feelings, the reactions, were nearly always the same—the wonderment, the sighs, the disappointment that the room was so crowded, the painting so modest, so small.

Cutting back over to St. Cross Road by way of the Lamb and Flag Passage, I entered the park at South Walk, passed the Cricket Pavillion, then looped my way south along Thorn Walk until it curved north again, along the river, where I found a bench in the shade overlooking the water and the large green meadow called Mill Pond Mead.

Now the sky was mostly clear, there was a light breeze blowing from the east, and, but for the occasional jogger, I was completely alone. The city—I could hear it as a murmur, a hum—seemed pleasantly far away.

Resting there, it struck me that the best strategy for finding Richard, for completing my work in Oxford, would be to return to the China Centre that afternoon, then everyday until he appeared, as he was bound if not certain to do. That resolved, I felt better. I read for a while, checked the email on my phone, then texted my neighbor and colleague, Debo, who was taking care of my cat. He himself had spent three years in England, when he first left Nigeria, first in Oxford, then in Reading, Brixton, and Crawley. He'd asked me to bring him a bag of Rhubarb & Custards, if I could find them, the popular red and yellow candies he'd enjoyed while he was here.

On my way back to my hotel I decided to sit for a spell on the steps of the Clarendon Building on the chance that I might see Richard again, catch a glimpse of his long gray hair. Finding a spot on one of the lower steps, I settled myself amidst the other tourists taking a break there. It was as good a place as any from which to watch for him.

While I couldn't see the Porter's Lodge from there, I was well-positioned to see him if he happened to come that way, say, to work for a while at Balliol College, to shop in the Covered Market, or to browse the books at Black-well's. Of course, if he came from the other direction, from Cornmarket Street, I'd be clean out of luck.

Yet so what? It was all a crap-shoot in the end, a matter of dumb luck, blind chance. Who knew? With all these people, Richard could sit down right beside me and I might never know it.

At that hour of the day the air felt close and humid. I adjusted my socks; I checked my phone. I had no faith that I would see him today. The truth was, my heart was not in it: I really didn't care, and for a moment I pictured myself in the gardens of St. John's, fast asleep beneath my favorite tree.

Try as I might to think like Mary, I found it hard to get used to the number of tourists here; surely something had changed in recent years, for I had no memory of such people, such crowds. Had they—wherever they were from—suddenly become wealthier, more curious, more daring? Or were they merely more restless, fretful, less happy with their lives and prospects at home?

I thought about the young woman I'd seen with Richard yesterday. I wondered if I'd recognize her were to see her alone and narrowed my eyes to consider the passing women, though, now that I tried, I could scarcely remember her face.

There were lots of young people, students mostly with matching t-shirts and backpacks, being herded like sheep along the densely packed streets. An elderly couple in shorts and plastic sandals had sat down beside me and were arguing companionably about something in the guidebook they'd just purchased, something about the nearby Bridge of Sighs.

Amused, I did my best to recall my first impressions of the city, when I arrived here years before. I remembered feeling awkward, conspicuous, that my clothes and habits were not quite right, so that in the days and weeks that followed I'd made a study of the locals here, of the men and women my age passing in out through the various college gates.

Oddly now, I didn't feel conspicuous at all. There on the crowded steps, I felt common, invisible, all but indistinguishable from the people around me, no matter their accent, their features, their clothes. The feeling was strange, the lightness, the anonymity; I didn't know what to think of it, and for a moment I closed my eyes, listening with a kind of rapture to the secret clamor of the city, when I was startled by a familiar voice.

"Jacob, is that you?" In horror I opened my eyes. I couldn't believe it: it was Richard again! Standing at the bottom of the steps, he was looking right at me. "What the hell are you doing here?"

I was so flustered to see him I couldn't even stammer, only stared at him, amazed.

"Let me guess: Mary sent you to spy on me, didn't she?"

"Spy on you? No, of course not!" I cried. "Why in the world would you say such a thing?"

"Because it's true, isn't it? It's that Quaker-like face of yours, Jacob. You've never been good at lying. But never mind," he said, clutching my hand and pulling me to my feet. "I'm happy, very happy, you're here."

What followed passed so quickly, with such little time for reflection, that that night I had to pause, before entering my hotel, just to find my bearings, my feet.

Upon spotting me on the steps of the Clarendon Building, Richard had taken me straight to Balliol College, where he'd introduced me to what had seemed like everyone he knew. I'd grinned, I'd shaken hands, I'd drunk cup after cup of tea, where we'd sat chatting with his various colleagues there, I couldn't say how many, in a dingy little office overlooking the Master's Garden.

They'd talked mostly of things I couldn't follow, things I didn't understand, teasing each other, nodding their heads, sometimes laughing out loud, so that I'd exhausted myself with smiling. When at last they'd asked me about my writing, my research, I'd scarcely had the energy to tell, to speak.

From there, upon the suggestion of one of Richard's friends, we'd made our way en masse to The Bear, a dark, low-ceilinged pub, just a short walk away, where we'd crowded ourselves around a low little table with pints of ale, toasting each other, the heavens, toasting the barman, the waitress, the cook. One man, a lecturer in archaeology with an ugly little beard, had talked for what had seemed like hours about the troubles he'd been having finding a particular part for the engine of his beloved Facel Vega, the same brand and model in which the writer Camus had been killed when his friend and editor lost control of the car.

As some of Richard's friends had found themselves hungry after all that drinking, we'd piled into a taxi and made our way to the Cherwell Boathouse, a restaurant they'd all seemed to know, the man with the little beard selecting a table for us by the water, then ordering ham hocks, lamb rump, and seam bream. And of course lots and lots of wine.

It had proven to be a lovely evening, there by the river. Once fed, once sated, the men had turned inward, grown thoughtful, discreet, so that by the time we'd left them at the empty restaurant they'd embraced me as a colleague and friend.

My hotel room had cooled off nicely again, so that for a time I stood at the open window to enjoy the early morning air. What a strange, unsettling day it had been. I scarcely knew what to make of it, what to think of Richard, about his treatment of me. I'd never seen him so gregarious, so solicitous, so kind.

I thought of the food and wine, heard again the clinking of dishes, saw the lights on the river and the empty, tethered punts. The evening—as I thought of it now—seemed as charmed, as ethereal, as a scene from a novel or film.

Yet something wasn't right. I felt it in my gut. In all the time we'd spent together I'd never once had a chance to speak with Richard, with Richard alone. It had seemed he was always telling a story, serving food, pouring wine, or chatting with someone else, with the steward, the waiter, with the charming sommelière. Seated at an angle across the long, broad table from him, the most I could have done, had I not been so drunk, would have been to study his behavior, to have watched him for fissures, for cracks.

He was off to Sheffield tomorrow morning to meet with a man about a project they were working on. He'd said he'd text me as soon as he returned.

And he'd said something else, something about a reception, if I remembered correctly. He'd told me I wasn't to worry, he'd take care of my clothes.

Finding my phone, I texted him at once to thank him for the evening, for introducing me to his friends, and to ask him about the reception he'd mentioned, about which he'd offered only the sparsest details.

It occurred to me to tell Mary that I'd seen him today, but I knew I'd have to lie, for I could never tell her I'd been discovered, that he knew that I was here.

I felt surprisingly alert, for the hour, and considered what to do. I could read, I could try to write, or I could just lie there in bed. Eventually, with the right music, I'd feel drowsy and sleep.

Plumping the pillows behind my head, I stretched out my legs and sighed.

Tomorrow I'd be on my own again. I might visit Blenheim Palace, I might rent a car and see the Cotswolds, I might hop the train to Stratford or Bath. I could do anything I liked.

Yet, hard as I tried to get excited about the options, none of them appealed to me. What I wanted, a desire that overwhelmed every other thought and feeling, was to ask Richard about the young woman, to confront him at last about the nature of his relationship with Mary. Surely he knew how she suffered, how, each day, she twisted and turned. By now he understood how she felt about his frequent trips, about having to sleep alone at night, about raising the boys on her own. He knew the demons that wracked her brain, that made her shrewish and hateful and cold. Of course it pained him, it must; after all, he wasn't a sadist. He could never be that cruel.

I decided that, instead of renting a car or hopping the train, I'd pick a restaurant or pub just outside the city and walk there, as I used to do with my friend and fellow, Ellen Martin. I did a quick search online and found a walk that appealed to me at once—a six to seven mile walk along the Oxford Canal from Jericho to Wolvercote, then back along the Thames. In Wolvercote, just past Altman's Bridge, there was a 17th Century pub called The Trout. It was there I'd have lunch.

I knew little about the Oxford Canal and read a short online history of it before switching out the light. Designed by a man named James Brindley, it was built by the Oxford Canal Navigation Company to provide a link with the coal-fields up north, as well as with London to the south, via the Thames. Five feet deep and sixteen feet wide, the canal and its towpath had reached Wolvercote in 1788. Dull, densely detailed, the description was exactly the sort of reading I liked most before bed.

Eyes closed, I tried to imagine the traffic on the canal in the days when it had served as a highway for the region—the tumult and noise, the watermen and navvies, the horses, donkeys, and mules. I was thinking of the long, slow journey from the north, of the farms and forests and clouds, when I drifted off to sleep.

I was up and showered by seven a.m.. I checked my phone: there was no reply from Richard. What's more, there were no texts from Mary. Not a single one.

It was strange not to have heard from her, I reflected uneasily, as I made my way toward St. Michael's to get a coffee, when I recalled the dream I'd had about her last night, about her and her father, about her as a girl by the sea.

Her father had shot himself in his car one day, in the parking lot at Tilden Beach, just minutes from his childhood home. She'd remembered the look on her mother's face when she'd returned from school that day, the wintry smell of the air, the light—and on the ironing board, in the middle of the kitchen, a heap of her father's good shirts.

Just seven at the time, she'd loved him dearly, her father, and had sat for hours, in his absence, in his old bergère chair, sometimes thinking, sometimes holding her breath until she felt her head and chest would burst. His heart had failed him, she'd been told. Like a clock it had simply stopped ticking, had quit.

It was only years later that she'd learned that his heart had not failed him at all, that finally, fatefully, it had served him quite well.

The letters to her father—all three of them—were brief, written by hand on company stationary by a man, an actuary, named Stan. She'd found them in one of her mother's boxes. Restrained, curiously formal, the writing was at points so stilted by longing she could barely read it, could barely whisper the words: *I received your letter, many thanks. Have you tried the whiskey I brought you? The wind is howling down the chimney tonight.*

It was hard to shake the dream, to free myself from its tendrils, so that I still felt vaguely apprehensive by the time I reached Jericho, the trendy neighborhood in the northwestern part of the city, where, according to Mary, Richard liked to stay when in Oxford. From there, it was easy to pick up the towpath near the end of Walton Well Road.

Shaded for long stretches, in parts nearly overgrown with bushes and flowers, the path was crowded with walkers and cyclists, and with people—women mostly—walking their dogs.

Narrow boats of every sort were moored along the way, some for hire, some for sale, many neglected, abandoned, considerably the worse for wear.

I was puzzled not to have received any texts from Mary this morning and wondered vaguely whether or not she'd heeded my words.

As I made my way north toward Wolvercote, I admired the backs of the many old house across the canal, with their gardens, boathouses, and docks, on one of which a withered old woman was sitting with her dog before a television.

The house in which Richard sometimes stayed was the last in a row on Southmoor Road. It was easy to find, having examined it, at least the front of it, on the internet last night. The backyard was beautifully tended with roses, ferns, and delphiniums, the boathouse immaculately refurbished as what appeared to be a studio, guest room, or study. On the dock, beside the open door, was a pair of teak-colored chairs, between which, on a little blue table, someone had left an empty glass and a novel, face-down.

Was Richard staying in the little boathouse? I wondered, craning my neck to get a better look at it. I could picture him there; it would suit him just fine.

He'd always had an easy, chameleon-like way of adapting to circumstances, no matter how strained or unseemly. I'd seen it at lectures and parties, in their apartment with Mary and the boys, and perhaps, most notably, in our recent travels together in southern China, a memorable, if often taxing adventure over the course of which nothing had seemed to faze him—the filthy hotel rooms, the broken toilets, the overcrowded train cars and buses. Even when exhausted, when we'd been traveling all day, when for hours we'd had nothing to eat but scallion-flavored crackers, he'd found a way to joke and tease me, to make a trifle of my impatience, my pique.

Again I wondered: was it possible, after all these years,

that Mary was right about him? I pictured the woman I'd seen with him yesterday. She'd seemed evidence enough. Still, there was a part of me, a significant part, that simply refused to believe it, that couldn't accept the notion that a man like Richard would stoop to something so crass, conventional, so patently banal.

Yet how else to explain the rumors I myself had heard about him, over the years—about him and certain colleagues, about him and certain students.

I remembered the first time Mary'd told me she was thinking of leaving him. I'd found her in her office overlooking Claremont Avenue, a stack of essays on her desk. It was late in the day, just before the holidays, December. She'd been meeting with students since noon, a task, one she'd long insisted upon, that had clearly taken its toll on her.

As usual I'd made us some tea, which we'd sipped for a time without talking, when, at length, setting her cup on the windowsill, stained by years of such rings, she'd said, "Every day he lies to me—about big things, certainly, but about little things, too, about things that hardly seem worth the trouble, the time, piddling little matters like leaving the toilet seat up, like eating my yogurt, like using the last of the stamps in the drawer. "And Richard's not the only one. Not by far. My editor lies, my friends lie, and my colleagues—everyone of them lies, every hour, every day!"

she despaired, indicating, with a flourish of her hand, the half a dozen offices outside her door. "I see the way they lie about their lives, here at work and online, especially online, the way they lie about their spouses and lovers, about their families, their vacations, about their diets, their classes, their friends. Understand, I'm as bad as they are; I lie to them, too. I have to. I could never let them in.

"And on and on it goes," she added, peering out the window at the cold, anemic sky. "Just now I found myself lying to one of my students, a pert, ambitious little thing. I couldn't help it. Only minutes before you arrived, I was telling her how insightful I'd found her last essay, even as I knew (and knew she *knew* I knew) that she was lying to me, that in fact she'd plagiarized the bulk of it, but also— and this is the part that really stings—it was clear to me, as she sat here before me just now, hands folded primly in her lap, that she knew I knew what she thought of *me*—of my class, my clothes, of my remarks about her work. Mind you, she was perfectly polite: she smiled, she thanked me. I was nothing to her, there was nothing I could do."

The path ahead was clearer, with fewer pedestrians, more open to the sky. I spotted what—by the map on my phone—must be St. Margaret's church, its steeple rising high above the treetops on the other side of the canal, passed quickly under Aristotle Lane, then found myself alongside some trap grounds, as I discovered they were called, a ragged expanse of reed beds and scrubland criss-crossed with boardwalks for birders and other naturalists.

What was it that still prevented me from believing Mary, from trusting what she felt? For as long as I'd known her I'd trusted her instincts about everything—about politics and literature, about music and art, about *people*, especially about people. She'd had only to say something and I'd believed it. What now was different? What if anything had changed?

Of course she herself had changed. It was something I'd *sensed* rather than known—at least in any objective, empirical way. True, her hair was different, she was thinner, more sinewy, there were wrinkles around her eyes and lips. But none of that was actually telling, germane.

The change she'd undergone, the real change, had happened elsewhere, within her, in the dark, unpublished regions of her brain. It was often enough just to watch her as she fed the boys, as she washed the dishes, as she talked with Richard on the phone. That was when one saw it, at least a glimpse of it, an intimation of something darker and strange.

Again I thought of Richard. I knew he loved her, that he'd never *wish* to hurt her. Alone with me, he'd always spoken fondly of her, as if of something consummate and fragile and rare. I couldn't recall even a single occasion when he'd reproved her in my presence—not a joke, a slur, not even an allusion to something unpleasant she'd said or done. When he spoke of her at all, and there were times when he spoke of her at length (of her work, her compassion, of her patience with the boys), it seemed it was often as of a foil to his own more feckless self.

I remembered a story he'd told me once, a story she'd told him when they were first dating, about an occasion in college when a friend of hers had pulled a prank on her. The friend, who at the time had been dating Mary's former boyfriend, had thrown her a party for her birthday to which she'd invited everyone they'd known. At the end of the party, which apparently had gone well, her friend had given everyone a bag of party favors, which they were not to open until they got home, in each of which, as it turned out, she'd tucked a photograph, a fairly blurry photograph, of Mary lying naked in the sun.

As Richard had told the story to me, his features had undergone a change, a change so subtle I might have missed it, had I not been watching him closely. His lips had tightened, his eyes had darkened, turned flinty, opaque. For a time his words had seemed to fail him, when, through his teeth, he'd remarked, as if it had explained it all, "I love her, you see?"

It was nearly noon by the time I reached Wolvercote. As towns go, it was small, deserted, not much more than a single wide thoroughfare called Godstow Road. While reading about it last night, I'd been surprised to learn that it was mentioned in the Domesday Book of 1086 as *Ulfgarcote* ('cottage of Woolgar' or 'Woolgar's place').

It was by means of Godstow Road that I would find my route back to Oxford along the Thames, which meandered its way south along the western edge of Port Meadow.

Yet first I needed some lunch.

Built hard by the river, with a large flagged patio, The Trout Inn had come highly recommended by virtually everyone who'd eaten there. I ordered a pint of bitter and a plate of the gammon, fried eggs, and chips. The place was pleasantly uncrowded, so that I remained seated there, with my book and coffee, long after my meal was done.

The ending of *Primera memoria* proved far more stirring than I'd expected, the final lines so affecting, so lyrical, I'd had to read them again:

> The arch of the veranda stood out against the haze, the sky barely illuminated by the early light rising behind the mountains, where the charcoal burners would be sleeping. Borja threw his cigarette on the floor, and impelled by some force we

rushed at each other, and we embraced. He started to cry. (It was punishment, because he had always hated Manuel. But I loved him, didn't I?) I was icy, rigid, and I held him against me. I felt his tears run down behind my neck and into my pajamas. I looked out on the garden. Behind the cherry trees I could see the fig tree, white in the early light. And there was the cockerel of Son Major, its furious eyes like two buds of fire. Upright and shining like a handful of lime, crowing stridently in the breaking dawn, crying out perhaps in the name of—who knows? how should I know?—some mysterious lost cause.

I set the book down and for a while just listened to the river, and to the murmuring of the other guests around me, my mind, my body, still pulsing with the impressions of that stirring final scene.

As soon as I started back to Oxford, I was waylaid by a construction project on the other side of Godstow Road, so that, to reach my path along the river, I had to follow a detour through a large, empty pasture in which there stood, without signage of kind, what looked to be the remains of an old stone church. When I searched it on my phone, I discovered it was in fact the remains of an old abbey, Godstow Abbey, reputedly the final resting place of Henry II's mistress, Rosamund Clifford or 'Fair Rosamund', which had ceased to function as such in 1529, during the notorious Dissolution of Monasteries under Henry VIII.

I couldn't resist taking some photos of the ruin to send to Mary; I thought she'd find it interesting, but decided not to send them after all. Instead, I sent her a quick note about how much I'd enjoyed *Primera memoria*. As she'd described it in her dissertation, years ago, it was indeed 'a great unruly book'.

The journey back to Oxford proved even milder, more peaceful than the walk to Wolvercote had been. Across the river, beyond the pasture and the distant line of trees, a pall of thick gray clouds had risen high against the blue, quickening the leaves in the trees and bushes around me.

I walked swiftly, hardly thinking at all, so far it seemed from everything I knew, when before I realized it, I was back in the center of town.

Shortly after I'd showered and changed my clothes that I received a text from Richard. He apologized, said something urgent had come up, so that he'd be unable to meet me before the reception tomorrow night, but that I was not to worry. First thing tomorrow morning, I was to go to a shop called Ballroom Emporium, just off St. Clement's, and ask for an old Scotsman named Duncan, who'd be expecting me. He'd take care of everything, Richard assured me. Once dressed, I was to meet him at the Centre at six.

I found the whole thing maddening, not to mention presumptuous. He'd never even asked me if I wanted to go, which—now that I thought of it—I devoutly did not. I'd never liked receptions, nor fancy gatherings of any kind, and dreaded the thought of the cocktails and chatter, of the music, hors d'oeuvres, and silly evening wear. Why hadn't I declined the invitation? Why hadn't I just said no?

I discovered, on my laptop, that the reception tomorrow night was to be held for a Chinese installation artist named Lin Tianmiao, before which she was scheduled to give a brief talk about her latest project, now on display at the Tate. Her art, what I could find of it online, was strange, disconcerting, consisting mostly of textiles and thread. Her first major work, *The Proliferation of Thread Winding*, was a mixed media installation in which a bed was filled with 20,000 needles linked by threads to 20,000 cotton balls, a television, and a video player. It had been conceived as a way of showcasing the labor of the now millions of women in China who made thread into cloth. I would like to have seen it in person.

For the rest of the evening I toiled away on my book at

the small painted desk by the window. The idea for the project, now so substantial, so sure, had come about by chance. One day, some years ago, while there in the Limousin doing research on the local Communist-led resistance to the Nazis, I'd met an elderly man, a shepherd, in a cafe in Aixe-sur-Vienne who'd mentioned to me in passing—I couldn't recall what we'd been talking about—the massacre at Oradour-sur-Glane. He'd been a child at the time of the attack, he'd told me, scratching his whiskered chin, yet his memory of the day was vivid, almost preternaturally clear. He remembered seeing smoke in the western sky and being told that Oradour was burning.

From one of the folders I'd brought along with me, I took out a book called *Petite Histoire d'Oradour-Sur-Glane* written by a local historian named Albert Hivernaud, which I'd purchased, along with some postcards and trinkets, on one of my many visits to the ruins. In the book, as in the now all but innumerable recountings of the tragedy, there exists a consistent tension between the desire to clarify the cause of what happened, to get to the root of things, and an imperative that it remain a mystery, forever unexplained. Writes Hivernaud: "Still today, despite the efforts of investigators and historians, all that we know for certain is the identity of the troops who carried out the massacre."

It had been by means of such accounts, I argued, that the massacre had become detached from its historical context, that is, decoupled from the truth of what happened, from the fact that the destruction of the village was not simply a massacre of innocents, another example of Nazi barbarity, but a deliberate reprisal for the villagers' support of the Resistance fighters, the *maquis*, and for their practice—rarely mentioned—of sheltering Jews. It was my contention, variously phrased throughout the book, that the commemoration of Oradour-sur-Glane is at heart the story of how, since the war, the incident has been emptied of its political particularities and thereby universalized as an example of ultimate victimization—an archetypal atrocity that now stands as a symbol for the suffering of France itself.

I skimmed a few more pages of the book, a text I knew well, considered the familiar cover with its grainy photograph of 'La lanterne des morts', then replaced it in the folder.

It was a lovely evening, the sky an even darker, stranger blue. I thought about the various ways, throughout history, that nations have commemorated their wars—their triumphs, their failures, their dead. The case of France, of its humiliation by the Germans during World War Two, was a striking and unusual one. Indeed its response, in the years immediately following the war, marked a turning point in the history of national grieving. Whereas, in the wake of World War One, France's commemoration of the conflict had been largely conventional, consisting primarily of the erection of 'monuments aux morts' in virtually every town square, from Lille to Marseille, from Strasbourg to Bordeaux, its response to the debasement and destruction of the Second World War had proven fundamentally, *necessarily*, different.

Beginning in 1945, the French commemoration of war had shifted radically from the traditional cult of the dead, of those killed in battle, often far from home, on cold and foreign soil, to a vigorous and unprecedented effort to preserve the sites and traces of the destruction itself, *les lieux de mémoire*. The reasoning was clear. The Occupation—with its anger, shame, and deportations, its traitors, spies, and informants, its betrayals, concessions, double-crosses, and vendettas, its guerrilla warfare and territorial fragmentation—had effectively blurred the distinction between home and front. How then to mobilize a beaten nation, to turn such suffering, such anguish, to gold?

It was General De Gaulle who'd devised an answer, a way to recover the pride and dignity of France, first, by conflating the two World Wars into a single heroic narrative, and second, by diverting the nation's attention (as well as that of the world) from the disgrace of its defeat and collaboration to the innumerable sites, throughout the country, of German violence and depravity. With its remoteness and simplicity, Oradour-sur-Glane was the perfect choice for a *village martyr*. SOUVIENS-TOI.

I woke the next morning to three new texts from Mary. To my relief, she'd decided not to go away with the boys, a decision of which I'd made no mention in my replies.

Drunk as I'd been, I'd made the mistake last night of telling her I'd finally seen him, Richard, in the produce aisle at Sainsbury's. She'd wanted to know everything about him—what he'd been wearing, what he'd been shopping for (what was in his basket), and how he'd looked to me, how he'd *seemed*, so that what had started, in my mind, as a comforting, even generous lie had spiraled quickly into an elaborate work of fiction, a farce. He was shopping for coffee and tomatoes, I'd told her, to which, at the end, he'd added a bottle of wine (Bordeaux), a box of cereal, three small bananas, and a half a dozen custard tarts. For some reason, I'd dwelt particularly on his clothes, on his pants and shoes, and on his shirt, a white broadcloth shirt which he'd worn with the collar open and the sleeves rolled back.

I'd gotten so caught up in the story, in my determination to sound convincing, persuasive, that I'd gone to the ridiculous length of telling her that, at one point, in Sainsbury's, as Richard was standing in line for the cashier, he'd struck up a conversation with the security guard by the door, an elderly man from Trinidad who'd told him in passing that he was the nephew of V.S. Naipual's favorite barber in Port-of-Spain!

I remembered I'd thought about telling her more—about his hair, his posture, about the patchy gray stubble on his chin, but had decided against it for fear of the questions such descriptions might raise.

And after that? she'd pressed me, at length. For surely I'd followed him. To the house in Jericho? Or to somewhere else, some address she didn't know?

I'd told her the only thing I could think of: I'd followed him straight to Balliol College, where he'd vanished with his groceries through the gate.

On a whim, feeling restless, I'd decided to take the bus to London, a little more than an hour away, to see the flower market on Columbia Road. It was something Celeste and I had planned to do together but had never managed to get there.

While seeing it on my own proved somewhat disappointing, I spent what remained of the morning there, pressing my way through the thick market crowds to admire the stalls with their colorful, sometimes exotic array of flowers, herbs, houseplants, and bulbs.

Feeling strangely elated, I called Mary's brother, Ian, to see if he could meet me for lunch, but he didn't answer his phone. Instead I took a taxi to Bloomsbury where I wandered through the leafy old neighborhood, as Virginia Woolf might have done, noting this and that, crossing Tavistock Square, Russell Square, then pausing briefly before the British Museum to admire, through the railings of the tall, castiron fence, its fluted columns and pediment, before making my way to a nearby bookshop where I bought a book of poetry called *Music for the Dead and Resurrected* by a Belarusian woman with the extraordinary name, Valzhyna Mort, which I read with absorption in the adjacent cake shop until it was time to catch the bus back to Oxford.


The reception was in full swing by the time I arrived at the China Centre the next evening. As it turned out, I was among the most formally dressed of all the guests. I felt like a clown and angrily searched the crowd for Richard, who was nowhere to be seen. I was making my way to the bathroom when I spotted the artist, Lin Tianmiao, chatting with a wealthy-looking couple by the stairs. With her short-cut hair and plain, frank face, she was listening to the woman, a lanky, blonde in a sparkling green dress, with an expression I'd seen before on the faces of certain nurses and nuns.

Once finished in the bathroom, I made another round of the guests, but there still was no sign of Richard. I helped myself to a drink and a miniature samosa, then wandered my way past the Wordsworth Tea Room, when I spotted him at a table on the lawn out back, chatting amiably with a group of dark-suited Chinese men, who appeared to find him amusing, grinning, shaking their heads, and laughing out loud in a way that made the other guests turn in wonder or censure to look at them.

He rose at once upon seeing me, vigorously shook my hand, then pulled out a chair for me beside him at the table, briefly interrupting his joke or anecdote only long enough to introduce me to the men, whereupon he continued talking with the same passion, the same now bold, now histrionic zeal.

Richard, I was not surprised to learn, had met the guest artist years before, at a party in New York. Apparently, they'd hit it off, so that she greeted me with a warmth and candor that spoke volumes about her affection for Richard. She was smart and funny, delightful. Had it not been for the other guests vying to have a word with her we might have talked there all night.

It was Richard who'd suggested we all go for a late-night meal at a Turkish-Mediterranean restaurant he knew out on Cowley Road. As there were too many of us to fit into a single taxi we piled into two of them instead. Richard made a brief effort to squeeze into the first taxi, the one in which I was seated, but was forced to join the others, including the artist, in the other, so that I was left grinning helplessly, for the duration of the ride, with five of the Chinese guests.

The restaurant was dazzling inside—crowded, noisy, beautifully furnished, and filled with the smell of grilling meats. When the waiter was seating us, I tried to secure a place near Richard and the artist, but was forced, by the press of the Chinese guests, and by the proximity of the tables, to sit at the opposite end.

The restaurant manager, as well, seemed to know Richard—shaking his hand and clapping him on the back so that, in what seemed like minutes, in about the time it took me to have few sips of my beer, the table was covered with food and drink, with bottles of wine, with shawarma, kebabs, lamb ribs, lambchops, and prawns, as well as with a variety of meze, little dishes of hummus, olives, and cubed feta, of dolmas, beans, seasoned yogurts, and baba ghanoush.

It was delicious, all of it, but the music was so loud that I could hardly make out a word of the conversation at the other end of the table, at least a part of which, in deference to the Centre's director, must have been carried on in English.

I was tired and eager to get out of my clothes, so that, just as they began discussing the prospect of whiskey and desserts, I slipped out the door.

The night was warm, even balmy, as I made my way west along Cowley Road. It wasn't a neighborhood I was familiar with, so that I walked slowly, examining the different restaurants and shops. There was a dazzling variety of small businesses, offering food and services in Arabic, Hindi, Hebrew, and Turkish. There were barbershops everywhere.

I realized it was silly of me to have imagined I'd have the chance to talk with Richard this evening, that I'd have even a minute with him alone. Still, I'd enjoyed the food at the restaurant, as well as my conversation with the artist, Lin Tianmiao. Hearing her talk about New York had made me strangely sentimental.

I was startled from sleep that night by the buzzing of my cell phone. It was just after 2 a.m. Thinking it was Mary I answered in a panic, only to discover that it was Richard, a contrite, drunkenly apologetic Richard. He was sorry, deeply sorry, he hadn't had the time to talk with me that evening. He'd not anticipated having to spend so much time entertaining the Chinese guests. The only way I was able to get him off the phone was to accept his apology and to agree to meet him at the Pitt Rivers Museum the next morning at ten.

The truth was, I hadn't accepted his apology, not at all, for I knew he hadn't meant it. What he'd told me suddenly seemed typical of him, but another string of errant, specious words.

Unable to sleep, I switched on the light by my bed. Why was I here? Had I no dignity, no pride, no basic self-respect? Richard and Mary had been using me for years; I'd always known it. They'd pushed and pulled me, they'd cheered and coaxed me, they'd flattered my failings, my fears. That they'd never meant to hurt me was no comfort at all.

BY THE TIME I ARRIVED at the museum the next morning it was nearly half past ten. I found Richard pacing the foyer inside.

"Good morning! I thought you'd stood me up," he remarked, with a grin. "I hope you're not still mad at me."

"Mad?' I replied in the same bluff tone. "Why in the world would I be mad?"

I thought I saw a flash in his eye, a recognition of sorts, but then he clapped me on the back. "All's well then—good! I have something I'd like you to see."

As usual he was causally, if impeccably attired. Over the years, he'd adopted what I could only describe as a more European style of dressing, an appearance at once more formal than that of his American peers and somehow more sporting, satisfied, more plainly, devoutly, at ease. Certainly, he'd never *looked* American—whatever that meant. His footwear alone was distinctive: handcrafted Italian leather shoes and boots, which he ordered, when in

London, from the same small shop. While he rarely wore a tie anymore, his shirts—of linen, poplin, and twill—were stylish, elegant, almost pretentiously well-tailored, well-made. In my loose khakis, short-sleeved shirt, and scuffed old wingtips, we must have seemed a curious pair.

The museum, located within the Natural History Museum, at the back of its main court, was a vast dark space cluttered with closely ranked glass cases, each stuffed to capacity with artifacts, large and small. I hardly knew where to turn, there was so much to consider, to see.

Richard knew the place well and led me swiftly between the cases, stopping briefly at one filled with elaborate silver betel nut slicers from India, which he loved, at another labeled 'Charms against the Evil Eye', and at still another, a longer, flatter case, crowded with antique lamellophones from all around the world.

He'd already been twice to see the special exhibit, he informed me, by the way, an introduction to traditional Evenki cosmology called 'Baeye dunne toktan' or 'Man is but a speck of dirt'. On display, in a series of flat glass cases, was a wondrous assortment of maps, masks, hide drums, drum beaters, textiles, calenders made of horn and mammoth tusk ivory, as well as a number of colored Russian engravings of Evenki shamans—clearly the products of a European eye and hand.

Yet for all his excitement about it he was impatient to move on. The exhibit he really wanted me to see, part of the museum's permanent collection, was a display of Japanese Noh masks, arrayed in a tall, well-lit case against one wall.

They were old, some of them very old, he told me, crouching to consider a particular mask in the lower left-hand corner. "This one here's an *onryo* mask, the mask of a spirit or ghost," he told me, cocking his head and smiling. "I've seen them before in Japan." The mask revealed the face of a man in agony, his skin a ghastly pallor, the mouth a rictus of pain, the eyeballs ringed terribly, inhumanly, in gold. Directly beside it was a greenish-gray mask depicting the face and spirit of a drowned man.

Yet it was the *onna* masks, the eerie white masks of mostly young and middle-aged women, that seemed most to intrigue him. "What's striking is how much they look alike," he exclaimed, as if newly struck by the fact. I squatted beside him to better see what he meant. "Have a look at these ones here," he instructed me, indicating a row of the chalky, white masks. "Upon first glance one can hardly distinguish them, they're so much the same. Yet to the trained eye, the *Japanese* eye, they're different indeed! You see, in traditional Noh plays the age and emotional state of a woman was often indicated by the state of her hair. See there? The masks representing innocent young maidens don't have a single hair out of place. By contrast, the loose strands painted on these other masks," he said, gesturing at three, more ashen-colored examples at the end of the row, "were designed to indicate the spirit of a woman who is older and somehow mentally disturbed, tormented by jealousy, sorrow, or rage."

As he spoke I listened carefully, even watching his lips in the effort to understand him, to grasp the import of what he was saying. He seemed—as he often did—to be saying something else.

"Conventionally," he explained, "it was believed that the best actors actually *became* the spirit of the masks they wore, the masks revealing, as if by magic, their deeper, truer selves. Look again," he instructed me, pointing to the *onna* masks. "As neutral, as lifeless, as they seem here in this case, the modeling of the features is in fact exquisite, deceptively complex, relying as it does on the subtlest asymmetry to reflect an extraordinary range of emotions with but the slightest movement by the actors. It was common, before a performance, for an actor to sit before a mirror and study the mask they were to wear until they became one with it, with the character they were to play. How else to explain their power, their force?"

Despite myself, and for all my desire to interrupt him, to confront him about the woman I'd seen him with at the bus stop, I found myself enthralled by his talking, by his description of the great Noh masters (of Umewaka Minoru, Sakurama Banma, and Kita Roppeita, the 'giant with a small body'), of the music and costumes, and of the various *kata*, or movement patterns, that ultimately defined the acting, the art. His words and delivery were so charged, so compelling, that a group of visitors, tourists from Germany, had amassed themselves around us, eager to look at the masks as he spoke.

It was the way he often talked, even when alone with one, when he was trying to be helpful, when he was trying to be clear and succinct, as when a student stopped him in the hallway after class to make some finer point about the previous night's reading; or when (in a cafe or park or in the back of the crosstown bus) a stranger interrupted him to inquire about the book he was reading; or when, in the cool, quiescent galleries of the Metropolitan Museum (to choose an occasion on which I was actually present), he overheard a young man in a fitted tweed jacket say something erroneous to his girlfriend about one of the museum's recent acquisitions, a 13th Century 'apparition painting' of a monk mending his robes in the sunlight. For Richard, everything was connected, everything was a part of a larger, more mysterious whole, so it that it mattered little where one started, one would find one's way in.

Only when we were back outside, when we were seated with a coffee at the little stand out front, did he pause to look at me. He smiled, I thought he might tousel my hair, when he said, "So what are you doing here, Jacob? Surely you haven't come all this way for the pleasure of my company."

Somehow I'd not expected the question—to find the focus, the onus, on me. I said the first thing that came to my mind. "Who was that young woman I saw you with yesterday?"

"Young woman? I know lots of young women," he replied, with a smirk. "I'll need you to be a little more specific."

His glibness made me angry; I felt the blood rush to my face. "You know damned well who I'm talking about. The woman at the bus stop with you, the one with the blunt cut hair and the fancy sunglasses. For God's sake, Richard, are you having an affair?"

For a moment he looked at me, a strange, searching look, when ever so slightly he tilted his head. "What do *you* think?" he replied. "Do you think I'm having an affair? Tell me, Jacob. You're my friend. I'd like to know what you think."

"What *I* think?" I replied. "This has nothing to do with me, with what I think."

"Nothing to do with you? That's funny. I think it has *everything* to do with you."

"What are you talking about?" I snapped. I felt a bead of sweat trace a course down my back. "This is about you, Richard, about you and Mary. It's always about you and Mary."

"Then why are you here?"

Staggered, nonplussed, I said, "You know why I'm here."

"I do? Then why am I confused?"

"Because you're not confused, Richard. You've never been confused a day in your life!"

He smiled thinly at me, his lips white. The response, it seemed, had hit home, but somehow I didn't feel good about it.

Surreptitiously, I watched him as he took a sip of his coffee, uncrossed his legs, then crossed them the other way. He cleared his throat as if to speak but said nothing.

I didn't like where this was going and blithely looked about me, hoping to alter the tenor, the mood. A couple passed us on their way into the museum, followed by a boy on his bike. The air felt hot and humid.

Finally, well in possession of himself, he said, "You love Mary, don't you?"

"Love her? You mean, as a friend?" I snapped, unable to master my tone.

He was about to say something cutting, I saw his lips quiver, when he thought better of it. Instead he nodded, he grinned. "Sure, Jacob, as a friend."

"Well then, yes. Of course I love her. But you know that already."

He made a soft, dull, humming sound with his mouth, then added, "Yes, you must love her very much to have made this trip for her. I wonder: would you have done the same for me?"

"For you? What a silly question. I have no idea."

"I mean, think about it," he said, gently replacing his cup on its saucer. "What if the situation were reversed, what if I were the suspicious one? Would you have spied on her for me? Surely women can be unfaithful, too."

Briefly, I studied his expression; his face—ever familiar—was strange. I had no idea what he was thinking. Was he mocking me, toying with me? It certainly seemed so, and for a moment I gaped at him. I felt angry, helpless; I had yet to find my footing with him and for the moment I hesitated to speak. *Order and method, the tongue says.* Order and method.

Ignoring his question, at least for the moment, I sipped my coffee, when in turn sipped his, dabbing his mouth, then crossing his gangly legs.

The silence between us had become unbearable, when an Australian couple sat down at one of the tables beside us and for a moment I watched them with relief as they examined the purchases they'd made in the gift shop—some greeting cards, a pair of butterfly tea towels, and a colorful tin of lemon crisp biscuits.

It was Richard who spoke first, his voice scrubbed clean, so that I had no idea what was coming next. "You've known me for a long time, haven't you?"

"Yes, I suppose so," I hedged, scowling at the bitter taste of the coffee.

"I'm just sorry it's come to this," he remarked, with a sigh. "I mean, you sitting here right now. Under these circumstances. If only I hadn't seen you yesterday."

I heard him chuckle, a chuckle for my sake, it seemed, for he smiled when I looked up at him. "It's odd, while I was waiting for you this morning, I was thinking about this guy I knew, this friend of mine from college, who used to play this game with me," he said, as if changing the subject. "We'd be sitting in a diner or cafe, it might be late, it might be first thing in the morning, it made no difference to him, when he'd point to one of the customers in the place, usually with the fork he was using, his mouth full of egg or sausage or toast, sometimes merely pointing with his elbow, his chin, say, to a young woman seated with her bedraggled mother in a booth in the corner or to a man with tattoos eating pancakes at the end of the counter or even to one of the waiters who'd paused in the midst of clearing a table to consider the people passing by in the street. "He'd called it, 'What's Their Weakness?'. That was the name of the game."

At that point he'd paused. I could feel his eyes on me.

"The challenge, of course, was to choose a person at random, a stranger, and see how long it took you to identify their weakness, that cardinal fault or flaw, that overriding source of anguish or shame, the mere touch of which would have them weeping on their knees. Of course, there was no clear way to verify one's claim, it was only a game, after all. One had to be convincing."

Flustered, my heart racing, I sensed what was coming next.

"Now picture yourself in that diner, Jacob, there beside my friend. If I was the person to whom he'd pointed one day, what might you have said?"

"I wouldn't have said anything," I replied, shortly, "because it's a stupid game. A cruel and stupid game."

"Yes, perhaps," said Richard at once, a look of amusement on his face, "but what would you have *thought*? After all, it's not as easy to control one's thoughts."

"Richard, what do you want? Where are you going with all of this?"

"Nowhere, really. I'm just curious about what you think."

"You mean about you? What I think about you?"

"Yes, about me, about Mary—about *everything*."

"Like what? What do you want to know?"

"Like, what was it that finally convinced you?"

"Convinced me?"

"Yes, what was it that finally convinced you she was right about me, that made you drop what you were doing and travel all the way here, to Oxford, on her behalf? I'm just curious to know what she told you, what it was that tipped the scales in her favor. I know how persuasive she can be."

"It was nothing, nothing particular. She simply asked me to do it, and as I had no other plans I said yes."

Chewing his lip he nodded his head. I watched him for a moment, doing my best to anticipate his next move, when, in an altogether different tone, he said, "I told you about the book I'm writing now, the one about the painting by Shih T'ao?"

"Yes. What about it?" I said, impatiently. "You know you still haven't answered me."

"Yes, I know. I promise I will," he replied brusquely, for clearly his mind was elsewhere. "Do you remember the painting itself?"

I remembered a figure on a precipice looking out at the folds of some distant mountains. "Yes, I think so," I said.

"You might find it hard to believe, but the first time I saw the painting I hated it. It unsettled me; what I felt was *excluded*. I felt it at once, that I'd been shunned, forsaken. I felt I'd been tricked."

"By the painting?"

"No, by *life*, by life itself: by my parents, my teachers; by Mary, my colleagues, and my students. Even by my boys, though surely I couldn't blame them: You see, I'd myself had been tricked."

At a loss I stared at him, annoyed by his incessant paltering, his equivocation, yet he seemed hardly to see me, to be aware of my presence at all.

"At first…at first when you look at it," he whispered, as much to himself as to me, "the painting appears to depict little more than a man, a scholar-artist with his guide or servant, gazing off into a remote and mountainous landscape, I've seen dozens of the kind before. Yet with time, if one is patient, other details and dimensions begin to emerge, for there is much more to the painting than meets the eye. Like the poem, for example. The calligraphy. Do you remember it? Initially one is hardly aware of it, as a part of the painting, though it occupies most of the right-hand side. One hardly sees it at first, as if one's eye, as if one's vision itself has been tricked.

"Yet there it is, and there it must be. That's its power, its *might*. You see, the poem describes a landscape quite different from the one before one's eyes, indeed an all but antitheticallandscape of ruined houses and city walls, of abandoned orchards and gardens, as if after a tempest, a war, of which, again, there are no signs in the painting itself, which, mind you, is not in the least bit realistic, but feels infused with ambiguity, with mystery: depths of pale ink wash; black lines blurred, smeared, bleeding; mountains dissolving into a faint blue haze. And there's so much empty space, so much mist and sky!"

He removed his sunglasses and looked at me now, or rather through me, his eyes dry and unblinking, like those of a person just risen from sleep.

You see, the space," he continued softly, half-closing his eyes, "the sense of space, of vast empty space, is expanded dramatically by the soaring perspective of the painting: the mountain ranges appearing one beyond another suggest the gazer is standing on a mountaintop of impossible heights. He seems a part of the emptiness itself, his body the same texture and color as the haze suffusing the mountain and valleys.

"Yet there's another suggestion, too," he remarked shortly. "There's a suggestion that the scene itself is less a rendering of an actual, physical landscape, than of the

147

gazer's own mind, an interior landscape we may possibly share with him when looking at the painting.

"Or else," he said, his eyes alight with the notion, "I've often thought of this, too, that the gazer has returned to some originary place where mountains are welling up into existence for the first time, alive and writhing with primeval energy, a place, a cosmic locus, as indistinguishable from the gazer's mind as it is from one's own…"

At that point, his voice trailed off, as though he'd suddenly grown weary of speaking, of the trial, the problem, of words, or else had simply lost himself in the vision of it all—the mountains, the ruins, the space. I looked at him, amazed. I couldn't think of anything to say and merely waited for him to speak again, to explain.

Yet he didn't explain: I'd doubted he would. Instead he examined the remains in his cup, then got to his feet and stretched.

"Come, let's walk," he said.

Still seated, I wanted to refuse him, to force him to answer me, to tell me the truth at last, but he'd already started toward the gate, so that I had no choice but to follow him.

Cutting through the Lamb and Flag passage, at the back of St. John's College, we made our way to St. Giles down which I followed him without speaking until we were standing beneath the awning of The Randolph Hotel.

"What are we doing here?" I demanded, intrigued, for suddenly he seemed anxious, unsure.

"I'd like you to meet someone."

"You're kidding me? You want me to meet the woman I saw you with the other day?" I shook my head; I could scarcely believe his audacity.

"Yes," he replied shortly, stepping aside to allow a porter to pass. "Her name's Diellza. She's my daughter, Jacob. She's here for a few days with her mother."

"Your daughter! Like hell she is. I saw the way you looked at her!"

To my surprise he took a step back from me, then wearily, as if disappointed, said, "I swear it, Jacob. She just turned sixteen!"

"Your *daughter*? Wait a minute. So you were married before?"

"No."

I looked at him, agog. "Then Mary's been right all along: you've been having an affair!"

"No…well yes, but it was years ago, many years ago, when I was teaching as a fellow in Berlin. I haven't seen her mother in ages."

I was incredulous. "And when were you planning to tell Mary? When your daughter got married, got pregnant?"

"I know, I know. I should have told her at once about Diellza. I myself only recently found out about her. It was Diellza who contacted me, about a year ago. November."

"Damn you!" I hissed, but loudly enough that a number of guests turned to look at us. "You know how Mary's been suffering. Months and months of anger and depression, of doubting herself, of thinking she was going mad. Nearly every day has been a torture for her. And you…you've said nothing! What the hell is wrong with you, Richard?"

"Listen, Jacob, it's not what it seems."

"Not what it seems? Why, it's *exactly* what it seems! You've been lying to her for years."

"What I mean is…here, sit down. What I mean is that I never planned it. I never set out to hurt or deceive her. Honestly. She's my wife, the mother of my sons. I tell you, I really never saw it coming." He struggled for a moment, unable to focus his eyes, when looking at me he said, "Understand, I'm not denying my responsibility here. It's terrible, really: Mary, the boys. It's ugly, painful, and sad. It's just that…it's just that it's more complicated than that, it's more than what it seems. Yet how to explain it?"

He was interrupted by the buzzing of his cellphone, apparently a text from his daughter, when he lead me across the hotel lobby where we stood for a moment by the elevators. "She's on her way down," he explained, before I could press him further. "I thought we could have some lunch."

I recognized her at once. Her hand was smooth and cool to the touch.

"My father's told me all about you," she said, wryly, as she preceded us into the dining room. "Such praise, I was beginning to think he'd invented you!"

She and her mother were staying in London for her mother's work, she informed me, once we were seated at a table in the window. While faintly accented, her English was good. She ordered the salmon, I the gnocchi, and Richard the Cornish plaice.

Pleased by the attention, and clearly enlivened by setting, she spoke eagerly about her friends and her interests, especially about her painting and writing. She hoped one day to visit New York.

The food was delicious, the time passed easily between us. I'd drunk my wine too quickly, so that when Diellza invited me to join the two of them on their trip to Stratford the next day, I'd hadn't the wits, the wherewithal, to say no. "It's not Shakespeare," she assured me, touching my arm, "but a contemporary play called *The Empress* about an Indian ayah. It's set in London, I think. At the time of the Raj. Apparently the critics love it!"

We'd just finished eating when, with what appeared to be some initial reluctance, Diellza told us a story about Richard, touching the rim of her wine glass, then touching her lips, a story she'd never told him or anyone before, one she was almost embarrassed to share with us, she claimed. "Ever since I first learned of you," she began, turning to look at Richard, "I followed you on the internet, you know, like a celebrity, like someone you can only know from afar. I studied the photographs of you and the videos of your lectures and talks, I read your books (what little I could understand of them), and I imagined scenario after scenario in which we met to talk—sometimes at a cafe, often at a restaurant I like by the sea." At that point she smiled. "I remember my astonishment the first time I heard you speaking Chinese. It was in a video I found online, how natural and effortless it seemed, how very much like you, somehow, though I scarcely knew you at all. I played the video over and over again, in my room, so that for weeks, before falling asleep at night, I imagined you speaking Chinese to me, it could be anything, a poem, a lecture, a basic conversation, as one might practice with a partner in class, *hello, how are you, which way to the palace, the beach*, it mattered little what you said to me, for I would understand it, you see, your language *our* language, our present and future, our means.

"Then, at long last, I saw you. I saw you in person!"

"You saw me in person?" said Richard. He seemed genuinely surprised. "You mean, last year, when we met?"

"No, in London, the year before that, in June. You gave a talk at the Royal Asiatic Society about the different conceptions of hell in ancient China. Remember?"

"Yes, of course I remember. And you were there?" he exclaimed, clearly troubled by the fact.

I'd never seen him like that. In his tone and affect he seemed positively wary.

"Yes, I wanted to see you in person, to see you before you saw me. I was hoping you'd speak Chinese. I wanted so badly to reveal myself, to tell you who I was, but I knew it wasn't the time or place. Perhaps you'll remember me: I was sitting in the front row, wearing a ruched red dress. After you'd finished talking I thanked you, I actually shook your hand!"

He screwed up his face now, as if trying with all his might to return to that evening, but to no avail. "I'm sorry, I hardly remember anything about the evening. It seems a long time ago."

"It's true, I shook your hand. You looked me right in the eye, I was certain you were going to say something, for you'd raised a finger as if you'd recognized me, or at least some aspect of me, perhaps a hint of my mother, who knows, when abruptly you turned to speak with someone else.

"It's funny, at the reception later, you accidentally spilled my drink! You don't remember that? You made sure I got another."

He shook his head; his face was pale. "I'm afraid the night is nothing but a blur to me."

"What about this?" she cried with pleasure, brandishing what appeared to be a large, long-stemmed cufflink. The decorative stone looked like jade.

"My snuff bottle cap! Wherever did you find it? I got it years ago in Hong Kong. It's really quite precious, quite old."

"You left it on the lectern that evening. I slipped it in my purse. I was certain I'd see you again."

"And here we are," said Richard, amazed.

"And here we are!" she said.


The drive to Stratford was a pleasant one, darkly, lushly green, as it had been raining lightly for days. Instead of taking the M40, Richard had chosen the more scenic route through the Cotswolds, by way of Witney, Burford, Stowe-on-the-Wold, and Chipping Campden.

As he drove, I studied the two of them from my place in the back seat of the car. I hardly knew where to begin in my thinking about Richard, about his affair, his daughter, about what I'd report to Mary when I returned. Surely she'd be devastated; she'd rant and rave, and she'd curse me for having doubted her, for having taken Richard's side, though in fact I hadn't, not at all. I'd simply withdrawn from them, from both of them; perhaps worse, I'd done nothing at all.

I had the advantage, where I sat there in the backseat of the rented sports car, with its silent air conditioning and plush leather seats, of being nearly invisible to them, screened from their notice, their apprehension, as we sped through the open countryside, as if in fact I wasn't there at all, as if in the end I'd decided not to join them on their outing and was back at my hotel, taking a nap on my bed. From my position I was able to study Diellza, as otherwise I would never have been able to do, to consider her profile, her mannerisms, the quick, sometimes anxious looks she flashed at her father as he drove, as well as to examine Richard himself, now all but a stranger to me—and all with the patience and impunity of a theatergoer for a pair of actors on the stage.

The illusion of being temporarily invisible to them was broken only now and then by the flicker of Richard's eyes in the rearview mirror. Once or twice I found him staring at me with a look so intense, so protracted, I was certain he'd crash the car, run head-on into a passing truck or bus, thereby killing us all.

What at length surprised me, in watching Richard with his daughter, the two of them chatting and laughing, at one point even singing a song together, the words of which he clearly didn't know, was the fact that I wasn't angry with him, now that I knew the story; I felt no rancor, no resentment at all. What I felt was a kind of pity for him, which feeling was new to me, at odds with him and our relationship, a pain, a sympathy, that somehow didn't seem right.

In short I was sorry for him, sorry that he'd betrayed his relationship with Mary, and with the boys, sorry that these moments with his daughter, in this car, on this dreary English day, had come as they had, at such a high and irremediable price.

It was Diellza's suggestion, once in Stratford, that we visit the cottage of Shakespeare's wife, Anne Hathaway. Together, we toured the iconic house, then wandered the gardens in which the roses were in bright and luxurious bloom, before stopping in for a quick lunch, before the matinee, at a place called Edward Moon.

The play was smart, diverting, in parts richly, variously staged, though I'd struggled at times to follow the plot. Based loosely on the story of an Indian named Abdul Karim who'd been selected as a servant to Queen Victoria, the story moved quickly between different settings, from Tilbury docks to Windsor Castle to the house of Lord Oakham, then back again to the docks and Windsor Castle. Diellza seemed genuinely to have enjoyed the production and spoke excitedly about it for most of the short drive back to Oxford. At one point, I'm not sure, I believe I fell asleep.

Upon dropping me off at my hotel, Richard asked me not to return to New York just yet. He said there was something more he wanted to talk about, to say. Unfortunately, he was scheduled to be in London the next day. Could I wait until Friday to fly out? There was a town he wanted to show me, a perfect English village called Iffley.

Of course I agreed to delay my return. I'd come this far; what could it hurt to stay a little longer?

Sitting in bed with my laptop on my knees, I decided that, while Richard was in London tomorrow, I would spend the day doing some things I'd never gotten around to doing while in Oxford. I'd visit the graves of C.S. Lewis amd J. R. Tolkein, check out Addison's Walk, and visit St. Margaret's Well in the nearby village of Binsey, a medieval well said to have been the inspiration for Lewis Carroll's 'treacle well', as it appears in *Alice in Wonderland*.

And tomorrow night I'd hear some music.

To my delight, I was able to reserve a ticket at Christ

Church Cathedral to hear The Raschèr Saxophone Quartet with The Schola Cantorum of Oxford perform a selection of works by the Estonian composer, Arvo Pärt.

The next day was bright, a breezy, a glorious day. All morning I'd been thinking about Simone, about the apartment she'd found for me for the summer, and about getting to know her again.

Instead of doing what I'd planned for the day, I took an early train to Cardiff, to Wales, to pay my respects to Celeste's father and to visit her grave. Her father, a retired ophthalmologist, lived in a cramped, two-room apartment above a bridal shop on the High Street. I'd spent an afternoon there with him and Celeste one day, she'd wanted me to meet him, for him to meet me, and I remember being struck by his reticence, by the odd, greenish pallor of his skin, and by his dark, unruly eyebrows, which seemed to twitch and tremble in place of his words.

Celeste had done most of the talking that day, she'd spoken for us, about our meeting on the train, about our work, and she'd spoken for him, too, in a way that had made me think she'd been doing it for years. The place was drafty and noisy in the summertime, she'd explained to me on her father's behalf, but the landlord was kind to him, an old schoolmate of his, and the view, well, if one leaned far enough out the window, one could see the castle on the hill.

I had to ring the doorbell of his apartment three times before he finally let me in. The apartment seemed more or less the same to me. The blinds were drawn, the television was on, there was a stack of old newspapers on the carpet by his chair. He offered me tea, which I declined, I feared it would take too long. Then he offered me a whiskey, he had a bottle of scotch he'd been saving, when at length, after a little more haggling, I agreed to a can of Theakston's Ale.

He didn't have the strength to accompany me to the cemetery, he told me, folding the morning paper in his lap, not anymore, though he was pleased that I myself was planning to go and pressed a wad of bills into my hand to cover the cost of the flowers.

As it was drizzling out, I took a taxi to Pantmawr Cemetery. I found her gravestone, beside that of her mother, on a shady, graveled lane called Byrn Adar. It looked different, the stone, somehow more natural, congruent. The grass had grown up around it and there was dandelion, a bright yellow dandelion, beneath the lines her father had had carved for her from one of her favorite childhood poems:

> As if I asked a common Alms,
> And in my wondering hand

> A Stranger pressed a Kingdom,
> And I, bewildered, stand—
> As if I asked the Orient
> Had it for me a Morn—
> And it should lift its purple Dikes,
>
> And shatter me with Dawn!

I slept for most of the train ride back to Oxford, so that I felt surprisingly rested that evening. After a curry at a nearby restaurant called Chiang Mai Kitchen, I made my way on foot to Christ Church Cathedral, where I sat in silent awe of the place—of the nave, the choirs, and the transepts, of the chancel vaulting and stained glass windows—until the program began.

The concert that evening was not what I'd expected, not what I'd imagined at all. It was louder, stranger, more disconcerting than anything I'd heard in years. That night, in my dreams, it had mingled queerly with the poems by the Belarusian woman I'd read: *Antigone. The Calibans. What is your alibi for these ledgers, these streets?*

As planned, I met Richard for breakfast at 9 o'clock the next morning, at a place called The Paper Boat Cafe by Folly Bridge. It was from there that we'd begin our walk along the Thames to the little town of Iffley.

He was talking on the phone when I found him in the garden there, a fairly animated conversation by the sound of it, so that I hesitated before joining him. Hunched forward toward the river, which ran directly beneath the damp, graveled garden, he didn't see me at first. I heard him snort, then mutter something, when scornfully, dramatically, he declaimed, "It's the part of a fool to say, I should not have thought!" It was only then that he noticed me, or sensed my presence beside him, and rose abruptly to his feet.

"Good morning!" he cried, clasping my hand. "I hope you slept well. Sit, please. I'll get us some coffee. The omelets here are delicious."

He had a lot on his mind. His meeting in London had not gone well: he'd traveled there, among other reasons, to meet with a gallery owner about writing the copy for an upcoming exhibition of paintings by the artist Wu Zhen, regarded as one of the 'Four Masters of the Yuan'. Though Richard was reputed to be one of the foremost experts in the field, the gallery owner had been unwilling, as yet, to commit himself.

"The man's an idiot," Richard scoffed, tearing off a piece of his croissant. "He can't even pronounce the artist's name correctly!"

He seemed to feel better for the aspersion, for having shared his disappointment with me: he sat back, crossed his legs, and sighed. The heat had finally broken, the air cooler, the sky mostly overcast with clouds.

I'd taken a bite of my omelet, when Richard, casting his eyes about the little garden, said, "Mary loves this place. She likes to spend the morning here when I'm working."

It was a curious remark, his use of the present tense, given that Mary hadn't been to England with him in years.

At once he realized his mistake. "Of course it's been a while." The realization startled him; he seemed surprised by the slip, so that for a moment he was quiet. A couple sat down beside us, a young Dutch couple in shorts and sandals, who, with their fresh and eager faces, seemed only recently to have arrived in the city.

"I miss those days," said Richard at length, wiping his mouth with his napkin. "We used to travel quite well."

As he seemed inclined to talk I said, "So, what happened? What changed?"

"I suppose I did," he replied bluntly, as if the question had never occurred to him before. "And of course she did. You yourself have seen the change in her."

"Yes," I began, giving him the chance to continue, to expand upon or at least to qualify his remark. When he didn't, when instead he took another bite of his croissant, I said, "That's it?"

"'That's it? What do you mean?"

"That's all you have to say about her?"

He scowled. "Listen. All I said was that she's changed."

Well of course she's changed! I've changed, you've changed, we've all changed. But there's a difference."

"A difference? In what sense?" he replied, so that briefly I wondered if he was kidding me, if he was being intentionally obtuse.

Nonplussed, I cocked my head. "Richard, the change in Mary, at least the change I've seen in her, is due almost entirely to *you*. You understand that, don't you?"

"Due to me?" I caught a flash of indignation in his eyes. "I've only ever wanted to love her, to support her. You know that."

"Perhaps, but that's not the point. The fact is she was right about you. You had an affair. You have a sixteen-year-old daughter whom she knows nothing about!"

"That's just it!" he said. "She has no idea about it. She doesn't know a thing." He shook his head, as if surprised at me, as if in fact I was the one being obtuse. "A secret kept secret harms no one. *Cui bono*? *Cui malo*? It's a matter of prudence, discretion. Truth be told, I'd prefer she never knew."

But she *already* knows!" I insisted. "At least, she's sensed it for years. She's said so to your face and you've denied it. Again and again you've told her, or at least have implied it by your silence, that she's mistaken about it, about you, that she's merely imagined it all. I tell you, the grief is killing her, Richard. She's thinks she's losing her mind."

With that he signaled the waiter for the check. He didn't look happy, brusquely paying the bill, before leading me out to the street.

Once over the bridge, we picked up the footpath that led south along the river. I was pleased to have gotten a rise out of him, at least to have given him pause, and followed him now at a brisk, if agreeable pace.

Among the narrow boats moored along the path there, I spotted the dark green one, called Morning Star, on which, for nearly an hour the other day, and from the other side of the river, I'd watched the man and woman patiently cleaning the metal fittings. At that time of day there was no sign of them, the cabin closed, the curtains drawn tight.

I noticed for the first time that Richard was a little pigeon-toed, that the heel on his left shoe showed greater wear than the one on his right. I was tromping along behind him, musing idly about his shoes, his gait, and about the wear and tear on my own old shoes, when, slowing down to look at me, Richard said, "Did you ever meet my father?" No? Well, I think you'd have liked him."

I couldn't remember ever having heard Richard talk about his father. Indeed so little did I know about his childhood that I used to joke with Mary about it, about his immaculate conception. Of his past, I knew of but a single relic in their apartment, a blurry, unremarkable photograph of him as a chubby little boy in a yard that Mary (in a fit of pique?) had hung on the wall beside the stove.

Mary herself could only draw me the vaguest, most cursory sketch of Richard's youth, of his life before she'd met him. If he wasn't secretive about his past, nor surely was he forthcoming, deftly changing the subject whenever pressed about his parents, his childhood, as if his demurral were simply a matter of humility, decorum, rather than a shield with which to cover some anguish or pain.

By contrast, he knew a lot about me, about my childhood, my parents, about my teaching and writing, about my diffidence, my love life, my dreams. He was particularly interested in my dreams, about which he'd inquire, whenever he had the chance, as if as a commonplace, a courtesy, as if wishing me good morning or asking how I'd slept.

His fascination had never struck me as strange; he'd always been interested in dreams, those of mine, those of Mary's and the boys', an advertence, an enthusiasm, at once personal and abidingly academic, discreet. Indeed one of his earliest books, one that had earned him a host of distinctions at the start of his career, was called *The Dream of Chinese Painting*, a book in which he'd examined the theme of dreaming in a variety of works by traditional or *guó huà* painters, using the much-hallowed text *The Duke of Zhou's Interpretation of Dreams* as a reference, a guide. He'd reveled in the ancient symbolism of things: in heaven and earth; planets and stars; mountains, rocks, rivers, and clouds; windows and doors; eyes and teeth; gold and silver; pearls and jade; spoons and chopsticks; dragons and snakes; fire and water; ghosts and coffins and death.

We walked a little further when Richard stopped to examine what looked like a gravestone at the side of the path. Erected by Queens' College in 1999 it read:

The Finish Stone
Torpids and Eights
in Memory of
Colin Cox
1945-1999
Oarsman and Boatman
dedicated to club and college
rowing
EN OPTIME FACIET

Something about the inscription made him smile. He turned to look at me, then past me, further on, at the place where the Thames meets the smaller, more tranquil Cherwell, on one side of which, on a wide green pitch, some men were playing cricket.

He said, "He never wanted for anything, my father. Not money, not power, not even respect. He was unlike the other fathers in the neighborhood when I was growing up. He had no interest in houses, in cars, in clothes. As far as I could tell, he never gave thought to beautiful women, though he'd occasionally tickled my mother when she was moody, an attention, an affection, that had always made her angry!"

He paused for a moment, as if allowing the memories to take shape in his mind, before adding, as if to compensate for what he'd said so far, "It's true, he liked baseball, my father, liked the Dodgers when they were in Brooklyn. He liked to watch a little golf on TV."

"Is that where you lived, in Brooklyn?" I asked him.

We'd resumed our pace again, so that I was wondering if he'd even heard me, my question, for he was talking about a German boy who'd lived next door to him, a boy who'd collected bottle caps and stamps, when all at once he replied, "Brooklyn, yes. Crown Heights. 904 St. John's Place. A nice middle class neighborhood back then, though I remember there were far too many Catholics for my mother's liking. She felt the Irish were not to be trusted."

"Who did she trust then?"

"No one really. Jews like us, I suppose." He shrugged his shoulders.

"So you were raised Jewish?"

The question made him chuckle. "No, certainly not! Apart from being vaguely patriotic, my parents didn't believe in anything at all."

"So what did your father do?"

"He worked in a bank, the Williamsburgh Saving Bank. Spent his entire career there, first as a teller, then as a loan officer. He liked to boast that it was the tallest building in Brooklyn. At least at the time."

"And your mother?"

"She took care of my aunt, my great aunt, Addie Dear. It was her house, after all. I think my mother was depressed a lot. She liked to bake and to talk on the phone. We had a big black phone in the kitchen then." He smiled warmly, when a scowl crept over his face. "All my life I've hated him."

"Your father?"

"I couldn't bear to look at him when I returned home from school. You see, he got injured one day, I was ten, a cabinet crushed his foot, so that he never worked again. I hated him for it, in the deepest parts of my heart. I hated everything about him: his foot, his chair, the baseball on the radio, and the bourbon—that stinking bourbon—on his breath.

"Yet there was something I hated even more, though it took me years to realize it. I hated the fact that he was happy, satisfied, that he never cursed the Fates, never turned bitter, never even complained. Imagine that: he never complained! Do you have any idea what that was like?"

Of course I had no idea what it was like and simply refrained from speaking.

"It's as if…it's as if he lived his whole life in parentheses," he told me. "Always smiling, obliging, always speaking softly, as if to apologize for having been born, for his very presence here on earth. Once, before he was injured, my mother took me to see him at the bank, she'd needed him to sign something, and I remember how small and sheepish he'd looked behind the high marble counter in his pale green shirt and wide brown tie, the way his glasses had flashed, the way, like a pigeon, he'd bobbed his spotted head." He groaned, rubbed his neck. "I couldn't stand it, his gurgling, his chatter, the blithesome, mindless bobbing of his head.

We walked a bit further, when, turning to face me, he said, "I used to do nasty little things to him, like hiding his glasses, stealing the batteries from his radio, and sprinkling salt in his whiskey. I couldn't help myself, I couldn't resist it. Understand: I didn't want to be cruel, I wanted to love him."

I watched him for a moment, his eyes flashed, his lips trembled, when shaking his head he said, "My father, he was just never willing to risk it. It wasn't so much a lack of courage, I think, as an excess of prudence, a surplus, a surfeit, of *sense*.

"He didn't suffer, my father. Not all all, that I could tell. For him 'sufficient' was plenty, enough." Briefly he paused, as if for the sake of timing, before adding, "He died three days after I moved to Taiwan. His doctor claimed he'd been perfectly fit."

As we continued along the river, we passed a number of university boathouses and some open fields, stopping now and then to look at the narrow boats moored along the way. At one point we stopped by the side of a water meadow, broken here and there by large, heavy-boughed trees.

"She's never trusted me," he said. "You know that, don't you?"

"Mary? Of course she has. I know she has."

He'd turned away from me, explaining, "Even at the start of our relationship it was clear she was watching me, assessing my behavior; she was always on her guard—for what I never knew."

"But that's what we all do when we meet someone new. We don't just dive in. We have to test the waters first."

"Yes, surely," he agreed, "but with Mary it was something else, something more, something stubborn, at points violent, eccentric, profane. Only recently have I been able to see it, to even begin to flesh it out with words. It's a wariness, a kind of vigilance, in her, that has always troubled me. After we moved in together, you remember our first place by the river there, even then, when it seemed we were very much in love, or at least that we should have been, I could feel it, the way she watched me, the surreptitious, sometimes conspicuous, way she appraised me while I sat reading the paper in the morning, washing the dishes after dinner, or taking a nap on the couch. It was naive of me, I know, but I thought that having a child of our own would change things between us, I was convinced of it, that the birth of Ivan would crack that shell of hers, that she would finally let me in.

"But she didn't. She didn't let me in. If anything we grew stranger, more distant to one another, more mutually unintelligible. She didn't like the way I held Ivan or the way I fed him. She hated the color I'd painted his room. And for months we slept apart; she couldn't bear to have me touch her."

"What about after Jack was born? I remember some very happy times."

"After Jack was born? Yes, there were some happy times," he agreed ruefully, "but by then it was too late. Little did I know, it was much too late."

I refrained from replying this time, lest I interrupt his train of thought. Instead we walked in silence for a stretch, a fairly long stretch, until we reached Iffley Lock. There were benches there, and for while we sat in the shade of a large willow, just across from the lock-keeper's cottage.

"When I tell you that Mary's never trusted me," he resumed, crossing his legs and hunching forward, "what I mean, what I really mean, is that she's never actually loved me. There's a difference you see: I can trust someone yet feel no love for them—but not the other way around. It doesn't work that way. It *can't*. To love someone means to trust them; it's a faith one feels, an all but religious intuition that they're who they say are, that they feel what they say they feel, that things—exceptions notwithstanding—are exactly as they seem.

"I remember the first time she followed me to work. She thought I didn't see her, indeed at first I didn't, but I *sensed* her, it was eerie, I knew I was being watched. She followed me all the way to my office that day. Even after I closed my door, she lingered by the stairwell, there at the end of the hall. I pitied her; I did. It broke my heart, the pain of it, the shame, but what could I have said?

"And there's more, Jacob. We'd hardly been married a year when she started going through my things—my briefcase, my wallet, my clothes in the closet and drawers. She did it regularly, if erratically, impulsively—when she thought I was sleeping, when I was out running errands, when I was working in my office or busy teaching a class. And of course she did it when I traveling, for then she could take her time, she could turn my study inside-out.

"Each time I was gone, she'd explore every nook and cranny of the room, searching the drawers in my desk, examining my files, pulling book after book off the shelves. She was typically thorough, even system-atic, in her approach. And she was careful, too, she has a memory for such things, a certain prudence and tact, though I could always tell she'd been there. Even in the air one finds clues.

"Mind you," he added, "I don't begrudge her the impulse, the instinct; one needs to protect oneself. What perplexes me, what troubles me still, is her persistence."

"Her persistence? You're joking, right? You know very well why she's been so persistent—because she's known all along she was right."

Frowning, Richard smoothed back his hair. "What I meant was that, in all these years, she's never been able to confirm her suspicions, never gotten close. She's told me so herself."

"Yes, but that doesn't change the fact that she's right, and has been so for years. However illogical it may seem to you, Richard, she *knew*."

He shook his head. "But, you see, that doesn't make sense. That's not when it started; it didn't begin when I returned from Berlin."

"What didn't begin?"

"Her behavior—the suspiciousness, the resentment, the paranoia. It began long before that, before Ivan was even born. I hardly noticed it at first, the clothes on the floor, the dishes in the sink, the brown untended, plants. She began to neglect herself, her hair, her clothes. She stopped eating, lost weight. She drank more, started smoking. For hours she'd hide away in our bedroom, ignoring my knocks at the door. I dreaded the tension between us. She slept poorly, suffered nightmares, and accused her sister of the most heinous, unconscionable things. Some days, many days, she'd just cancel her classes.

"Then came the strangest change of all, I'd initially failed to remark it, it would have seemed too silly, absurd. You see, I'm convinced—even now I hesitate to mention it—that, after years of working closely with me, she not only began to resent me and my work, the paintings and poetry, the panels, meetings, and lectures, but also Chinese itself."

"You mean, the language? That's ridiculous!"

"I know it sounds crazy, but hear me out. There came a time, long before my affair in Berlin, when suddenly she seemed to cringe whenever I spoke it. I was flabbergasted. She used to love it when I recited my favorite poems to her, when I sang her old nursery rhymes to ease her out of bed…"

"But Richard that's not accurate, that's not fair! All you're doing is describing how Mary is *now*, or at most how she's been for the past couple years. She hasn't always been like that. She *hasn't*. Remember, I too know her well."

A narrow boat was approaching the lock and I thought he might want to watch it pass through, I myself had never seen it before, but he rose to his feet. "Come, he said. "The town's just up the hill. The little church is there, the one I was telling you about."

I followed him across the lock, then up along a deeply shaded path through the trees.

There, upon an outcrop above the Thames, just beyond the rectory, stood the modest Church of St. Mary the Virgin. Built in the late Romanesque style, of a pale, locally quarried stone, it was notable, Richard informed me, as we followed a narrow path around the building, for its elaborately embellished doorways and façade. It was a favorite of his, the church, and almost always empty, as it was when together we crossed the threshold into the cool and ancient gloom.

Just inside the West doorway, in the first cell of the church, was the baptistry, in the center of which stood a large black marble font. The basin, I could see, was dry.

"I like to come here to think," he told me, as we wandered our way up the aisle, when he settled himself in one of the pews. Awkward as it felt I took seat beside him. "There's a kind of quiet here I've never found anywhere else. Sometimes it's like a ringing in my ears."

He was telling me about the original four-cell ground plan of the church, about the way the floor gradually rises from west to east, in the direction of the altar, when he stopped himself to say, "Believe me when I tell you that the changes in Mary that I'm talking about started a long time ago. It isn't any wonder you didn't notice them." Out of the corner of my eye I could tell he was looking at me, or at least had turned his face in my direction. "Close as you've been to her, Jacob, you could never have seen the changes I'm talking about, they were at first so fine, so subtle, so *strange*. You wouldn't have known what you were looking at."

I felt weary, impatient, for it was hard for me to believe him. "What do you mean? What changes are you talking about?"

He hesitated before saying, "There were times when we were having sex that she would fixate on my penis, fondling it it, squeezing it, even pinching it. Sometimes she studied it for so long that I lost my erection. What was clear was that she was looking for something—traces, evidence. I think she was looking for clues."

"Listen, Richard, I don't need to hear this."

"But you do!" he replied. "How else am I to convince you?"

"To convince me of *what*?"

"Of the fact that her anger and paranoia are not simply my fault."

"I never said they were *simply* your fault. The matter's obviously more complex than that. *She's* more complex than that."

"Exactly!" he said. "That's exactly my point." He sighed, sat back. "You know it hasn't been easy for me. Or for the boys. It's clear by the way they look at her sometimes that they're wary of her, of her moods, that they're afraid of the things she might do."

"That's insane! They adore her, Richard. They know very well how much she loves them!"

"Be that as it may, they're perceptive. Children often are."

"Which is to say what? That some days she's depressed, that some days she finds it hard to make sense of her life?"

"You know, I once found her unconscious at the kitchen table. You didn't know that, did you? I thought she'd killed herself, for she'd threatened it before. It turned out she'd only been drinking, nearly an entire bottle of gin. By the time I found her she was cold, her skin gray, she was hardly breathing at all.

"Mind you, things improved after Ivan was born. She stopped drinking, began eating well, she often took him for walks in the park. What's more she got back to her work. She wrote articles and reviews, she started teaching again. And for months she seemed happy, at peace with herself. And with me.

"Then it started all over again—the muttering, the sulking, the suspiciousness. She searched my things, she followed me to work, she left me angry, awful messages on my phone. She was taking a variety of meds at the time, a combination of antidepressants and antipsychotics, so that it was nearly impossible to know how to talk to her, to help her. For months, I was truly at a loss."

His hand was trembling as he adjusted his glasses on the bridge of his nose. I thought he might say something else, but instead he closed his eyes. As he breathed through his nose, I could see his nostrils gently flaring.

His words made me sick to my stomach. While certainly I could acknowledge that there were things Richard knew about Mary that I myself did not, there must be, I was deeply troubled by his portrait of her, which, for all the force of his description, just didn't ring true.

I thought of Mary, of Mary and the boys. Never in all my time with them had I feared for their safety, had I doubted her judgment, her love. That she'd suffered from depression and anxiety was hardly new to me, I'd known of it for years. Indeed it was often in her darker moods that she'd called me to talk, that she'd stood at the tall glass doors in their livingroom, gazing out over the park at the lights of East Harlem and Queens.

Over the years, as Richard had traced wider and wider circles in the world, I'd been drawn deeper and deeper into their lives, into the very fabric of their living, their days. I'd spent so much time with the three of them that, at points, the boys had come to feel like *my* boys, Mary my lover, my wife. I'd often spent the night in their apartment, when Richard was away, especially when Mary was busy, when she was tired or in her office working late. I'd fed the boys, I'd read to them, I'd put them to bed. Yet not for an instant had I ever questioned Mary's behavior as their mother. Even at her worst, there'd been a consistent clarity to what she'd told me, a grounding, a pattern, to the way she'd reasoned her way through her pain, that seemed woefully at odds with Richard's depiction of her. That Mary, *his* Mary, was a stranger to me.

Yet why would he lie to me? I wondered. Why would he invent such ugly, such compromising, details? It baffled me; it just didn't make sense. What possible motive could he have to justify such an elaborate deception, when—if in fact he'd been that unhappy—he could have asked for a separation, gotten his own apartment, he could have sued her for divorce?

I stole another glance at him, where he sat resting

in the pew beside me; his eyes were still closed. I'd never known him to be dishonest or misleading about anything. On the contrary, he'd often gone to extraordinary, often painful lengths to be truthful, objective, and fair. If he was frank with others, he was unsparing with himself, always the first to acknowledge his failings, his flaws.

I hardly knew what to think, to believe. What if he was right about Mary? What if the things he'd been telling me were true, a side of her I didn't know, that, in my love of her, my devotion, I'd been blinded to the gravity of her condition, to the facts?

The possibility was deeply troubling, and for a moment I couldn't focus, I couldn't breathe, and was on the verge of standing up, when, like punch in the gut, I remembered the note that Mary had shown me one day, which she'd found tucked between the pages of one of her books, a scrap of common notepaper on which someone, in a bold, if indeterminate hand, had scrawled the words: VILE UNSPEAKABLE CUNT.

Just then I heard a rumble of thunder, one loud enough that Richard opened his eyes and sighed.

"I don't know about you," he said, "but I could use a drink. There's a pub right here, up the street. We can sit outside unless it rains."

The pub, as it turned out, was just minutes away, in

the heart of the little town. We ordered a couple of pints then sat outside at one of the picnic tables ranged about the roughly cut lawn.

The sky had clouded over again. I was tired, almost desperately so, and sipped my beer, hardly tasting it at all. I wanted to return to my hotel, draw the blinds, and close my eyes. I wanted to tell Richard I didn't believe him, that he was wrong about Mary, that, no matter how he painted it, he himself was not the victim, such a claim was selfish, outrageous, absurd. I wanted to shout and scream, to take him by the collar and shake him.

"Why are you doing this?' I said aloud, before I could catch myself.

He looked at me askance. "Doing what?"

"This! This game you're playing with me. Ever since we met here you've been toying with me."

"Toying with *you*? Listen, you're the spy," he reminded me. "You're the one who followed me here to Oxford. I didn't invite you; I didn't ask you to come."

"Then what about Mary? Why are you doing this to her? She doesn't deserve it. I mean, the things you've told me—you know very well I can't verify them. Instead, you expect me just to believe you, to take your word for it."

He scowled, shook his head. "You're a grown man, Jacob. I'm not forcing you. You can think whatever you like."

"What I think, Richard, is that you're full of shit, that every day you shape the world to suit you—no matter the consequence to others, the price. The Mary you describe, she's nothing like the woman I know!"

"So you think you know her pretty well, do you?" Not for the first time, he seemed to be eyeing me from the other side of a fence.

"Well enough to know when I'm being conned."

He grimaced, drawing his lips tightly against his teeth. I watched him sip his beer, then wipe his mouth with the back of his hand. Fixing me with his pale gray eyes, he said, "Then you know she was raped."

I gasped. "Raped? Good God, I had no idea!"

"You mean, she never told you?" he cried in mock surprise. "I thought she told you everything."

"No, she never said a thing to me! When did it happen and where?"

"I don't know. Years ago, when she was sophomore in college. She said the man had tried to kill her, that she'd barely escaped."

I was flabbergasted. "I...I... How long have you known?"

"Since just after we got married. Understand, she herself never told me. A friend of hers did. At a party. She was drunk. She made me swear I'd never say a thing."

"So you've never asked Mary about it?"

"No. And I never will. How could I? What in the world would I say?"

Again I felt sick, like I might vomit right there on the grass.

"So what will you tell her?" asked Richard, at length. His tone—it made me look up at him—was smug, contentious. "Surely she'll want to know what you found out about me."

I shook my head. "I… I have no idea what I'll say."

"You could tell her the truth."

"The truth! What truth? I wouldn't know the truth if I fucking tripped over it!"

Exhausted, bewildered, we finished our beers in our silence. I pictured the bed in my hotel. Perhaps if I closed my eyes for long enough I'd find that it had all been a nightmare, an ugly, grueling dream.


I'd just gotten to my room when I received a text from Richard, apologizing for his abruptness with me. Lately— he couldn't explain it—he just hadn't felt himself.

To make it up to me, he invited me to dinner, the following night, at the house where he was staying in Jericho. Before I flew home he wished to clear the air between us, to make his amends.

I was inclined to refuse his offer, I was angry, eager to go home, I didn't want to see him again, at least not here, and waited until nearly nine that evening before I acquiesced.

I spent my last day in Oxford wandering the crowded streets, looking at books, and texting back and forth with Simone whom I'd be seeing—she'd offered to meet me at the station in Limoges—in less than three weeks.

Once showered and dressed, I hailed a taxi to Southmoor Road. For all the furor of the last few days, I felt strangely elated as I gazed out the window at the buildings and houses flashing by. Richard had had an affair, he'd finally copped to it, and affair from which had come a daughter, now twenty years old. While it was true I didn't trust him, he'd seemed genuinely contrite by the time he'd dropped me at my hotel last night.

I would tell Mary that. For what it was worth, I'd tell her how sorry, how afflicted, he'dseemed. Despite myself I pictured them happy again.

I arrived at the house on Southmoor Road at seven p.m. sharp. I was feeling hungry for the first time all day. Knowing Richard, he'd prepared something extravagant for me, with multiple courses, not to mention with multiple bottles of wine.

I rang the doorbell and waited. Briefly I heard voices inside, I thought I saw the curtains flash, when the door was opened wide.

"Ian, what are you doing here?" I cried with delight. It was Mary's brother, dressed in shorts and bare feet. He must have come up from London to see me.

"I'm living here," he replied, hugging me stiffly then urging me inside.

"You mean with Richard?"

"Yes," he replied, glancing first at Richard, who'd just appeared at the door, then back at me, and I was about to follow them into the house when it hit me.

"No!" I cried. I couldn't believe it.

Richard had seized me by the arm and was trying to to pull me into the house but I snatched my arm away. "You monster, you bastard, you son of a bitch!"

"Jacob, listen…"

"You and *Ian*, Richard? Who the hell are you?" I railed blindly, stumbling my way down the steps, when with a newfound horror I gasped. What had I been thinking to come here? What in the world had I done?

I scarcely remembered the walk back to my hotel. The next thing I knew I was at the airport, boarding the plane for New York.

It was raining lightly by the time I arrived at Mary's building on Morningside Drive. I found the elevator was still broken and climbed the three long flights to her apartment. The air in the hallway was hot, stagnant, so that for a moment I struggled to catch my breath.

I was about to ring the doorbell, I heard the television, I knew she was waiting just inside, when I hesitated. I considered my shoes, my bags. I pictured the kaleidoscopes I'd bought for the boys, the book and the Jaipur scarf for Mary, but I couldn't do it, I couldn't ring the bell. I felt a strange lightness in my head and limbs, a nearly feverish chill, and was about to remove my jacket when, in a flash, I was back in the bay with the bluefish and kingfish and muddy winter flounder. I heard my step-father's voice, heard the lapping of water against the hull, and I knew. I knew there was nothing I could tell her, nothing I could say, and might have wept at the realization had I not been so eager, so *happy*, to flee.

## Acknowledgements

First and foremost, I'd like to thank Marc Estrin and
Donna Bister at Fomite Press for their unwavering support
of me and my work. My debt to them is great.

I am grateful to the following authors for the inspiration
I drew from their work, from Juan Goytisolo's *Count
Julian*; Anna Maria Matute's *The Island*; David Hinton's
*Existence: A Story*; Sarah Farmer's *Martyred Village:
Commemorating the 1944 Massacre at Oradour-sur-
Glane*; Aatish Sateer's *The Twice-Born: Life and Death on
the Ganges*; Ellen Coon's "Possessing Power: Ajima and
Her Medium"; and Phillip G. deMaynadier's *Our Maine:
Exploring Its Rich Natural Heritage.*

As ever, I'd like to thank my good friends and colleagues:
David Gutierrez, Ivan Hageman, Hugh Himwich, Cynde
Moore, George Ovitt, Tina Ruyter, Gwen Pirtle, Melanie
Peterson, and James Wolberg. I am fortunate to know
you.

Finally, I'd like to thank my family: Linda Forcey,
Margaret Nash, Franklin Nash, Suzanne Nash, Isaiah
Nash, Ezra Nash, Kyra Schmoker, and my wife and
partner, Annie Nash, who enriches my life every day.

## About the Author

Peter Nash is the author of the novels, *Parsimony, The Perfection of Things, The Least of It*, and *In the Place Where We Thought We Stood*. He has also written a biography called *The Life and Times of Moses Jacob Ezekiel: American Sculptor, Arcadian Knight* and has co-authored a collection of essays called *Trotsky's Sink: Ninety-Eight Short Essays About Literature*. He lives in New Mexico with his wife and two sons.

Fomite

Writing a review on social media sites for readers will help the progress of independent publishing. To submit a review, go to the book page on any of the sites and follow the links for reviews. Books from independent presses rely on reader-to-reader communications.

**For more information or to order any of our books, visit:
fomitepress.com/our-books.html**

## More novels and novellas from Fomite...

Joshua Amses—*During This, Our Nadir*
Joshua Amses—*Ghats*
Joshua Amses—*Raven or Crow*
Joshua Amses—*The Moment Before an Injury*
Charles Bell—*The Married Land*
Charles Bell—*The Half Gods*
Jaysinh Birjepatel—*Nothing Beside Remains*
Jaysinh Birjepatel—*The Good Muslim of Jackson Heights*
David Borofka—*The End of Good Intnetions*
David Brizer—*The Secret Doctrine of V. H. Rand*
David Brizer—*Victor Rand*
L. M Brown—*Hinterland*
Paula Closson Buck—*Summer on the Cold War Planet*
L.enny Cavallaro—*Paganini Agitato*
Dan Chodorkoff—*Loisaida*
Dan Chodorkoff—*Sugaring Down*
David Adams Cleveland—*Time's Betrayal*
Paul Cody— *Sphyxia*
Jaimee Wriston Colbert—*Vanishing Acts*
Roger Coleman—*Skywreck Afternoons*
Stephen Downes—*The Hands of Pianists*
Marc Estrin—*Hyde*

Marc Estrin—*Kafka's Roach*
Marc Estrin—*Proceedings of the Hebrew Free Burial Society*
Marc Estrin—*Speckled Vanities*
Marc Estrin—*The Annotated Nose*
Marc Estrin—*The Penseés of Alan Krieger*
Zdravka Evtimova—*Asylum for Men and Dogs*
Zdravka Evtimova—*In the Town of Joy and Peace*
Zdravka Evtimova—*Sinfonia Bulgarica*
Zdravka Evtimova—*You Can Smile on Wednesdays*
Daniel Forbes—*Derail This Train Wreck*
Peter Fortunato—*Carnevale*
Greg Guma—*Dons of Time*
Ramsey Hanhan – *Fugitive Dreams*
Richard Hawley—*The Three Lives of Jonathan Force*
Lamar Herrin—*Father Figure*
Michael Horner—*Damage Control*
Ron Jacobs—*All the Sinners Saints*
Ron Jacobs—*Short Order Frame Up*
Ron Jacobs—*The Co-conspirator's Tale*
Scott Archer Jones—*A Rising Tide of People Swept Away*
Scott Archer Jones—*And Throw Away the Skins*
Julie Justicz—*Conch Pearl*
Julie Justicz—*Degrees of Difficulty*
Maggie Kast—*A Free Unsullied Land*
Darrell Kastin—*Shadowboxing with Bukowski*
Coleen Kearon—*#triggerwarning*
Coleen Kearon—*Feminist on Fire*
Jan English Leary—*Thicker Than Blood*
Jan English Leary—*Town and Gown*
Diane Lefer—*Confessions of a Carnivore*
Diane Lefer—*Out of Place*
Rob Lenihan—*Born Speaking Lies*
Cynthia Newberry Martin—*The Art of Her Life*
Colin McGinnis—*Roadman*
Douglas W. Milliken—*Our Shadows' Voice*
Ilan Mochari—*Zinsky the Obscure*
Peter Nash—*In the Place Where We Thought We Stood*
Peter Nash—*Parsimony*
Peter Nash—*The Least of It*
Peter Nash—*The Perfection of Things*
*George Ovitt—Stillpoint*

Printed in the USA
CPSIA information can be obtained
at www.ICGtesting.com
LVHW041922081024
793282LV00001B/30